RECLAIMED
BAGGAGE

RECLAIMED
BAGGAGE

KATIE O'ROURKE

Library of Congress Cataloging-in-Publication Data

Names: O'Rourke, Katie, 1978–, author.
Title: Reclaimed Baggage / Katie O'Rourke.
Description: 192 pages. – First edition. | Laguna Hills, California: Type Eighteen Books, 2025.
Summary: "A recent widow and retiree, who just so happens to be a perpetual liar, discovers she might have to change her ways if she wants to keep her family together—and if she wants a chance at romance with the honest man who recently entered her life." —Provided by publisher.
Identifiers: LCCN 2025930591 | ISBN: 979-8-992-04052-4 (paperback) | ISBN: 979-8-992-04053-1 (ebook)
LC record available at https://lccn.loc.gov/2025930591

TYPE EIGHTEEN
BOOKS

Published by Type Eighteen Books
www.typeeighteenbooks.com

Printed in the United States

Also by Katie O'Rourke

Unclaimed Baggage
Blood & Water
Finding Charlie
Still Life and Other Stories
A Long Thaw
Monsoon Season

Chapter One

"I have an early morning."

"Oh?" Barbara forces herself to the surface. She pulls the sheet tighter across her bare breasts, annoyed at herself for drifting.

"Don't get up." Sitting on the edge of the bed, he turns his back to her and pulls on his shirt. From this angle, she can see the bald patch at the back of his head. When they were both standing, he had been much taller.

Stewart.

And when they were lying down, well. She wouldn't have seen it then either, would she? Something makes her feel sentimental toward him, suddenly, like he's letting her in on a secret. She has an impulse to reach out and touch his broad shoulders with her fingertips, but he stands, shifting his weight as he shuffles into his shoes. Fast. Practiced. He's worn his loafers.

Barbara sighs. Stewart turns and smiles at her. "You look lovely. Just stay. I can let myself out."

She smiles back. She can't possibly look lovely—her hair somehow both wild and flat, her face smudged on the pillow—but she appreciates the lie. "You're sure?"

"Oh, yes." And she's grateful he leaves it at that. She tells herself she's grateful. She waits until she hears the bang of the front door, relieved she doesn't have to get up in front of him. She's been spared the indignity of exposure as she'd have tried to wrap all her sagging parts in a quick bathrobe apology.

She can't go back to sleep, though. This is her daughter's room. She still thinks of it that way, even though years have passed since the children left. There was no need to redecorate, hardly any reason to come upstairs at all. And she's always liked the delicate glass baubles Jenna had hung by the window.

Barbara walks naked to the bathroom at the top of the stairs, happily invisible without an audience. She can't bring a man into her bedroom, the room she shared with Bill. It's been eighteen years since he died. A lifetime: longer than they'd been married.

Not longer than they'd loved each other, though. The years they'd lost during life are more heartbreaking than the ones lost to death. She figures she has no power over death, but in life, there's only herself to blame.

Barbara flushes the toilet, stands at the sink, and forces herself to look. Her mascara has run halfway down her cheek. Lovely, indeed. She wonders, as she often does, what Bill would think of her like this. The pretty young thing he'd met on a beach. What she's become.

She used to lie about her age, claiming to be older. First, to get into the clubs, to meet the kind of men worth going with. She'd had a fake ID someone's older brother had procured. The photo looked nothing like her, but the bouncers never seemed to mind. Because of that ID she met her first husband, the first Bill. They ran off and got married the day after her eighteenth birthday. Moved to Ohio and welcomed Billy into the world before she had turned nineteen. Then the lie was for the rest of the PTA moms, so they wouldn't think she was a child; to seem respectable.

People used to say how young Barbara looked, an innocent compliment. Sometimes, lies didn't hurt anyone.

Her second husband, the real, beloved Bill, had been nearly twenty years her senior. They'd been married to other people when they fell in love. It was complicated, and divorce seemed like a big enough scandal. So, she chose not to correct the record. Eventually, she forgot which number she'd told people, and everyone stopped asking.

Except for the children, sometimes. She hedged. Once, Billy had called her vain. She'd laughed with Bill about that later. The idea that she pretended to be *older* out of vanity.

It had come out after Bill died, one of the smaller truths emerging into the light of his absence along with everything else. It hardly mattered then.

If Barbara were the sort of woman to get her lover's name tattooed on her body, she could claim there had been only one man in her life. Besides having the same name, the two men were nothing alike. The first Bill had controlled, demanded, and shamed. The second had loved, honored, and cherished.

Barbara leaves her blouse and slacks on the floor in Jenna's room. She'll get them tomorrow. She descends the stairs, puts on her comfortable pajamas, and climbs into the big bed, alone.

***

Barbara's had the same hairdresser since the summer after Bill died. She'd needed a change and didn't want to go to anyone who'd known her before, who'd look at her with pity. Her life was divided between *before* and *after,* and she found it was easier to deal with people who only knew the *after.*

Monique's catered to Black clientele, something Barbara hadn't realized for the first several minutes of her first appointment, all those years ago. It had dawned on her slowly; being the only white person in the room was not a common experience in New Hampshire. But once she'd sat down, she couldn't very well leave, and no one ever made her feel anything but welcome. That first haircut had been stylish, shorter than she'd been used to, and needing regular upkeep. Before then, Barbara had never had a regular hairdresser.

She spoke to Monique once every two weeks: deep, personal conversations, more intimate than the way she spoke to nearly anyone else in her life. It began to feel like friendship. She finally admitted to being a widow, but by then, it was no longer recent, and she'd never needed to be treated with kid gloves.

Monique meets her at her station and drapes a black cape around her. "Regular trim?" she asks, snapping the buttons into place.

"Sounds good." Barbara sets her glasses on the counter in front of her, pleased when her reflection becomes a blur.

"You know, we could do something different," Monique says, running her fingers through Barbara's sharp bob. "Something softer?"

Barbara squints at the mirror. She hasn't had long hair since she was pregnant with the twins. She had cut it herself, crying in a bathroom mirror in Ohio, the kitchen scissors sawing through angry fistfuls. She looked like a mental patient. Her first husband had chalked it up to hormones. These days, she keeps her hairstyle current, blunt, professional. It stops at her jawline and only needs a touch with a flat iron at the tips. She's not sure she's ready for *softer*.

"Just a trim," she says.

"You keeping busy?" Monique reaches for a purple spray bottle and spritzes Barbara's hair flat against her head. She knows better than to suggest a shampoo in the back. Who has time for such luxuries?

Barbara sighs. "Keeping busy is what old people do."

Monique shakes her head, insisting she'd meant no such thing. "I know you, that's all. How long ago was your retirement?"

"Six months." And three weeks, Barbara thinks. Monique had been at the celebration dinner in January. Jenna's idea, held at the Back Room with Sam and the kids. Julie had come down from Maine. Billy flew in after not being able to make it for Christmas. Monique had been the only guest who wasn't family.

"Does having so much free time drive you nuts?"

Barbara shrugs. Work had defined her for such a long time. When the kids were young, work was a necessity she derived no joy from. But after Bill's retirement, he helped her buy a small company where she could be her own boss. She sold air filtration systems for commercial spaces. She made presentations, managed salespeople, and wore smart suits with heels. She loved the travel involved. Now she was free to wear pajamas past noon. No one to notice.

"Ruby and I have been taking a yoga class this summer," she says, not really answering the question.

"Oh, how sweet. I love one-on-one time with the grandbabies." Monique is at least ten years younger, but already has seven grandchildren. Barbara only has two. Will is eleven and Ruby is five. Jenna had had such trouble conceiving the second time, it's unlikely there will be more. Julie divorced without ever having any. Billy's in his late forties and seems in no rush to settle down. When Barbara asks him about dating, he says he has no time, but all the doctors Barbara knows have managed to find wives.

"Ruby starts kindergarten in the fall, and I'll get her after school so her mom can work." Jenna runs family therapy sessions from her home office. Barbara doesn't think it's safe, letting her patients know where she lives, but Jenna swears she doesn't serve a high-risk demographic. Barbara thinks everyone is a risk.

"What about Will?"

"He thinks he's too old for a babysitter. He's starting junior high."

"Where does the time go?" The women shake their heads in unison and debate whether to wait until next time to touch up her roots.

In the end, Barbara agrees to come in next week for the coloring. She doesn't have time today. She's been packing her schedule full since January, and she only has an hour before the next appointment. She has time to go home, make a sandwich, and eat standing over the kitchen sink to spare herself from cleaning up crumbs later. She has a vision test at one o'clock. She's trying to fit in all those annual appointments she never had time for: teeth cleanings and mammograms. Basic maintenance of the human body is an endless chore that only gets worse as you age.

***

Barbara's cellphone rings as she reaches the car. She doesn't recognize the number and considers letting it ring and ring and go to voicemail. That's what Jenna would do. But Barbara's curious. If it's a telemarketer, she'll tell them to take her off their list. It gives her a little charge—lately, her only chance to feel authoritative.

"Hello?"

"Mrs. Shaw?"

"Yes, who's this?"

"My name is Lisa. I'm an emergency call agent from CarePlus. I'm sorry to inform you, but your mother has been taken to the hospital."

"My mother?"

"Yes, ma'am. Judy Flynn?"

"She asked you to call me?"

"Actually, your number is listed as an emergency contact. I couldn't speak to her before the ambulance arrived."

"What happened?"

"I'm not exactly sure. She seems to have fallen. The call button has fall detection, and we were alerted, but, as I said, I was unable to speak to her. Would you like the information for the hospital she was taken to?"

Barbara knows there's a correct answer to the question; in fact, she probably should have asked before it was offered. But something else is nagging. "She has *me* listed as her emergency contact?"

"One of them."

Ah. Barbara hates giving strangers personal information, but she sees no way around it. "Look, my mother and I don't really speak. I don't think she'd want me to show up at the hospital. You should probably call someone else on the list."

"I see." There's a long pause. Barbara imagines there isn't a call center script for this. Poor Lisa. "The thing is, ma'am, I tried all the other numbers, and nobody answered."

And then Barbara remembers: Jenna and Sam took the kids camping. It's the last week before school starts, and they couldn't afford to take them on a real vacation. Barbara offered to give them the money, but Jenna refused. Pretended camping was something she liked.

Who knew where Julie was? Nothing new there.

Barbara fumbles in her bag for something to write with.

***

It's strange, Barbara supposes, but the phone call doesn't alarm her right away. Her mother is too formidable to worry over. But she gets caught in beach traffic on the drive from New Hampshire to Maine and has time to think about what this fall could mean. Her mother is well into her eighties now, by all accounts still sharp, but cognition doesn't protect people from a heart attack or broken hip. And she remembers something the operator said: *I was unable to speak to her.* What does that mean? Had she been unconscious? Barbara hadn't asked then, and she can't ask now.

Barbara calls Julie's number the whole trip but gets voicemail every time. Julie's been living with her grandmother for the last few years since her divorce. The least responsible of Barbara's children, Julie is Jenna's twin, born second. They'd both been tiny, but Julie was smaller, got held back in school, and Barbara always thinks of her as the baby of the family. It's harder to imagine her looking after her grandmother than the other way around.

Case in point: Where is she now?

It's probably time to start thinking of putting her mother in a home, selling the house, not that it's Barbara's job to decide such things. Barbara hasn't been to Boothbay in more than thirty years. She wasn't invited back to the house after her father's funeral. She'd stood next to her mother at the cemetery, the two women locked in their own pain, not touching, not a word exchanged between them.

In the years since, they've spoken only when they had to, a forced civility, for the sake of the children.

But the children are grown now.

***

"Mrs. Flynn, your daughter's here!" The nurse announces this sunnily, entering the room.

Barbara stands back, sheepish in the doorway. Her mother turns her head to look at her with wide eyes. A figure who looms large in memory, she seems smaller in the hospital bed, older. Barbara tries to remember when they saw each other last. Was it Will's hockey game, or Ruby's dance recital? Sitting far apart to avoid forced interaction. "The girls didn't answer their phones," Barbara says in response to the obvious, unasked question.

The nurse looks back and forth between them, clearly taking note of the distance. "How are you feeling, Mrs. Flynn?" she asks, loudly, pulling her chart from the foot of the bed.

"Fine, dear, much better. I'd like to get back home."

"I know, honey, but the doctor explained earlier he wants to keep you overnight."

"I remember," the old woman snaps. "I'm just not happy about it."

"Noted."

"Nothing wrong with my memory."

"Also noted, and glad to hear it. You bumped your head when you fell." The nurse slides the chart back into place, her smile constant. "I'll be back to check on you."

Barbara steps into the room, allowing the nurse to get past her.

"I've left messages for Julie. Once she gets here, I'll get out of your hair."

"I'm sorry you had to make the long drive."

"It's fine."

A long silence fills the space between them.

"I'll probably sleep a little," her mother says, finally.

Barbara nods. "I'll leave you to it. Back later."

There are blue arrows on walls leading to the cafeteria, and Barbara doesn't have to speak to anyone for the next several hours. She grabs a table in the back corner and checks her email on her phone, calling Julie's cell every twenty minutes. She memorizes the cheerful message. She reschedules the eye appointment for next week, apologizing for the emergency.

She watches strangers wandering in by themselves or in groups, looking confused, shell-shocked, or unconcerned, selecting their egg salad sandwiches wrapped in cellophane, making polite conversation with the bored cashier, laughing or staring into space, lost in thought.

When Bill was sick, Barbara got used to spending time in hospitals. She can tell which people are here to visit a friend who gave birth, versus a spouse who's had a heart attack, or a child who's crashed a car and been in a coma for weeks. The joy or terror or resigned numbness is written all over their faces.

Barbara keeps to herself, eating a dinner she buys from the vending machine, looking too busy to be drawn into conversation or asked for directions. By the time she heads back to her mother's room, close to eight, the cafeteria is empty.

Her mother is sitting up in bed, watching the news. She mutes the television when Barbara enters the room.

"I haven't been able to locate Julie."

Her mother frowns. "She left before I got up this morning. They're working on a new house." Julie still works with her ex-husband, Rick, flipping houses. She swears they get along better now than when they were married.

"Do they usually work this late?"

"Sometimes. Or go out with friends. I called the house too."

Barbara sits on the edge of a chair, as though to lean back would be too much of a commitment, presumptuous.

"Well, I'm fine, as you can see. You needn't stay."

"I'll leave when Julie gets here."

"Don't be silly. You have a long drive. I'm sure she's—"

"I'm not going to leave until Julie gets here." Barbara says this more firmly the second time. "They're keeping you overnight. Do you plan to take a cab home in the morning?"

Her mother shifts in the bed, pulling the sheets tighter across her lap, sitting up straight. She sets her jaw and seems to consider whether this is the argument worth having. "Well, you might as well sleep at the house then. They put my pocketbook in the cabinet there. You can get my keys out."

Barbara remembers the thrill she felt as a girl whenever she was allowed in her mother's large pocketbook. The keys are on the top, fastened together with a gaudy plastic butterfly. She's surprised there are so many of them and must get instructions on which is the house key. She considers making a joke about her mother moonlighting as the high school janitor but ends up thinking better of it.

***

Thirty years, and she could still drive the back roads blindfolded and find her way. It's too dark to see the ocean, but she can smell it, and she can hear it. The sound of her tires in the gravel driveway has a crushing familiarity. The house hasn't changed or been updated in any significant way; black shutters contrast the still white paint. Inside, there are dark wood floors, porcelain bath fixtures, and large, patterned wallpaper from the sixties.

Barbara never thought much of the cramped house while she was growing up here, but it really is beautiful. It was built a hundred years ago by men who took time with details, nothing like the mass-produced, *ticky-tacky* little boxes she's lived in since. The old place wasn't fancy — one bathroom on the first floor, no air conditioner or dishwasher, and three small bedrooms on the second floor. The only thing setting the master apart from the others was the view of the ocean out the window.

Her mother had moved her bed into the office downstairs years ago, but still hasn't changed a thing in the upstairs bedroom she'd shared with Barbara's father. Their matching oak dressers stand on either side of the double bed: hers, short with a mirror, and his, eight drawers tall, once well over Barbara's head. She'd had to stand on her toes to reach the surface. Her father kept a dish of spare change there, whatever had collected in his pockets during the day. Sometimes she pilfered a shiny quarter, too young to have any real use for it, drawn in by the idea that it had a value. A mysterious lure.

Barbara decides to make up the bed in the spare room that was once hers.

***

At daybreak, Barbara sits at the kitchen table and sees Julie walking up the drive. She eyes her mother's car with suspicion. Does she recognize it? Perhaps she notices the

New Hampshire plates; it isn't Jenna's cranberry minivan. Julie picks up speed as she seems to put it together.

Pushing forty, Julie manages to make the walk of shame look good. Her long blond hair is tousled just so, her jeans are ripped at the knee, and she wears a white tank top with a yellow bikini top showing through with a sweater tied around her hips.

She throws the door open and finds her mother sitting incongruously in the kitchen. Her face is panic stricken, a wounded child. "Where's Grammy?"

Barbara stands and goes to her, ready for Julie to fall in her arms, a fantasy. "She's fine. Only a little fall. The hospital kept her overnight to be on the safe side." She reaches out, touching Julie's arm instead, and waits for her daughter to recoil.

She doesn't. Not physically. "Why are *you* here?"

"No one could reach you."

"Where's Jenna?"

"Camping. I'm not sure she has reception."

"And Mrs. McClure?"

Barbara returns a blank stare.

"Our neighbor."

Barbara remembers a woman in pink pedal pushers and a white tennis visor, planting bulbs in her front yard. Nearly forty years ago.

"Wow. I was last on a long list, eh?" Barbara means to make light of it but ends up sounding bitter. She returns to her seat. "I haven't heard from anyone."

"I was up the beach. Hooley had a bonfire. My battery died."

Barbara nods.

Julie sits across from her and puts her elbows on the table, face in her hands. Her shoulders shake.

"She really is fine, dear. She may have bumped her head, and they wanted to keep her overnight, but she should be able to come home this morning. I was about to head over."

"I'll go get her," Julie says, standing up.

"All right then."

"Will you be here when we get back?"

"It's probably best if I'm not. I think she's had enough of me.

Julie sighs. "Okay." Barbara watches her go before finishing her coffee in one gulp and rinsing the cup in the sink. Out the window, she can see the waves out beyond the grassy dunes. She gathers her things and hurries outside to toss them in her car, eager to have a walk along the beach before her mother returns.

The sand is cool on her bare feet; Barbara remembers racing to the water's edge to cool them during the summers of her youth. This morning is bright, but the chill is a reminder of the impending fall.

Barbara sits before she gets to the damp sand, not tempted to dip her toes in the frigid water. She knows it will be a struggle to get up again. Her hips, her lower back, her knees. At least there is no one to see.

This is where she met Bill for the first time, all those years ago. She'd been sitting much as she is now, thinking she was alone, when he walked out of the ocean toward her, his tan muscles dripping. His presence was disorienting, catching her off guard, immediately intimate. Their first conversation, and they were alone, and he was half naked. He told her he'd been working on his parents' roof all day, and the heat was making him crazy. She offered him lemonade and he stood on the back porch, refusing to come into the kitchen because his feet were caked in sand. He drank three tall glasses, tipping his head back and guzzling them down greedily, his Adam's apple bobbing.

He'd been wearing a wedding ring, as she had, but neither of them spoke of their better halves, not then, and not on the many other occasions they met that summer in various stages of undress.

***

Barbara hears her cell phone ringing as she's walking back to the car. By the time she fishes it from the pocket of her purse, it goes silent. She sits behind the wheel, and the phone rings again. She glances at the screen before answering. Julie.

"Hello?" Barbara tilts her head, pinching the phone to her shoulder as she puts the key in the ignition.

She can't understand a single word Julie says, and, also, she understands immediately.

Chapter Two

Over the years, Barbara has imagined what her last conversation with her mother might be like. Several romantic fantasies involved speaking at her hospital bedside. But not quite like this. Barbara can't even remember the last things they said to each other.

Certainly, she knows it could have been worse, considering all the hateful things that had passed between them. After James. Her turbulent, rebellious adolescence. The afternoon she returned from running off to get married years before, naively thinking the introduction of a grandchild would still her mother's tongue. The day she upset her father so much he had a heart attack.

You've killed everyone I've ever loved.

But those weren't the last words. No, the last words were generic, she can't recall what they were. It's pathetic and horrible in its own way.

***

By the time she gets to the hospital, Julie is eerily calm. She'll admit later Rick slipped her Xanax. He handles everything, looks up the address for the funeral home on his phone. Barbara feels redundant. She excuses herself to the bathroom, not needing to go. Once there, she goes anyway and spends several minutes sitting on the toilet, leaning her head against the stall. She thinks she might spend the afternoon there, if not for the entrance of a woman with a small child. Barbara flushes, washes her hands and dries them. All the while, she can see the child in the mirror, peering at her from beneath the stall door.

When she leaves the bathroom, Barbara turns left instead of right. She pretends she's wandering aimlessly, but she has an aim, and she finds it: the room where she'd last seen her mother.

It's empty now, and dark but for the light coming through the thin drapery. Barbara leans in the doorway, feeling silly, not sure why she came, what she thought she might find. She recognizes the impulse as sentimentality, and she's embarrassed by it. Obviously, they've cleaned the room. Julie already had her personal effects in a bag. There's nothing here.

"Can I help you?"

Startled, Barbara straightens and turns to see the nurse from yesterday. It already feels like long ago. She's forgotten her name—if she ever knew it. She blushes as the woman approaches.

"How are you holding up, dear?"

"I'm fine, really," Barbara insists, uncomfortable with endearments uttered by strangers, especially someone younger. "She'd lived quite a...life."

"Yes. It's always hard, but I hope that's a comfort," the nurse says. "She went peacefully, in her sleep. Isn't that how we all want to go?"

Barbara nods slowly. She certainly didn't wish her mother a painful death—she's not a monster, after all— but, somehow, the idea of her being able to release her grip on this earthly plane without some torment or regret rankles.

Barbara pretends to get a message, though she's turned off her phone. In the empty lobby, she turns it on and sees several texts from Julie.

Where are you?

I can't find you!!!

Meet us back at the house???

***

This time, Barbara knocks at the front door and waits.

Julie yanks the door open, then looks disappointed. "I thought you were Jenna."

"Is she coming?"

Julie nods, walks to the living room and throws herself face-down on the couch.

"She won't get here for a few more hours," Rick reminds her, as if she's a toddler with no sense of the distance between Manchester and Boothbay.

Julie says something that gets lost in the couch cushions.

"Can I get you something to drink?" Rick offers.

"I'm fine." Barbara sits in the navy-blue wingback. Her father's chair, recovered. It used to be brown.

Julie's right arm dangles to the floor, her fingers worrying the deep pile carpet. It's impossible to tell if she's crying.

Years ago, when Bill died, his son had come to town and made the arrangements. Barbara had gone with him to the funeral home—merely for show, a courtesy. He made all the decisions, and she'd been grateful. She hadn't cared about any of it: the casket, what he'd be wearing inside the casket, who would do what readings at the church. None of this mattered.

Now, Barbara isn't sure who will make the decisions. She's afraid to ask. What if they think she should be the one? Something of this import seems beyond Julie; most adult situations do. Perhaps everything will become clear when Jenna arrives.

Rick disappears into the kitchen to make sandwiches, reminding Julie she hasn't eaten all day. Barbara wonders if he always takes care of her this way, or if their dynamic is shaped by the day's loss. Julie has always had someone to take care of her. Growing up, Jenna held her hand and tied her shoes. Even when they seemed to grow distant in their teen years, Jenna covered for Julie, protected her from the judgment of others.

"I can help you with the mortgage," Barbara says.

Julie turns her face from the couch cushion. "What?"

"I don't want you to worry about making the payment."

"Oh, God." She lifts her dangling arm and presses the heel of her palm to her right eye socket. "I hadn't thought of that."

"Well, don't." None of the children realize Barbara's retirement has left her a good bit richer than she was before. When you own the company, retirement means selling it. She's only spoken of those details with the lawyer, but she can afford to pay the mortgage indefinitely if need be. Suddenly, she realizes the house must have been paid off. "Was she only paying taxes at this point?"

"*What?*"

"Either way." Barbara shakes her head. "Don't worry about it."

"I *wasn't!*" Julie snaps, sitting up. She gets to her feet and stomps out of the room without offering a shred of gratitude. Julie has always been the most temperamental of the kids. They'd gone years without speaking after Bill's death had outed a lifetime of secrets. Jenna had been angry, but stayed close, demanding answers. Sometimes this felt harder. Billy let her off the hook entirely; they'd never spoken about it to this day.

Barbara sits in the room by herself for a while, waiting for Julie to return, contrite. When she doesn't, Barbara decides to head home. She already has plans to see Jenna tomorrow. They'll take Ruby to the park for the last afternoon before kindergarten starts. She lets herself out without saying goodbye.

***

Barbara fumes on the drive home, thinking ill of the dead. It's her mother's fault, after all, that Julie remains petulant and immature. There had been a major crossroad in Barbara's relationship with Julie, and rather than being forced to work it out, Julie ran to the comfort of her grandmother, resulting in years of estrangement. A rift that would never fully heal.

Barbara's attempts to reconcile with her mother would end up creating a distance from her own children. Both daughters turned to their grandmother whenever they felt their mother had failed them. The house in Boothbay was an easy escape. Once they got their driver's licenses, their grandmother's house was a few hours away, close enough to avoid whatever was going on at home. Grammy always welcomed them with open arms. Barbara had never been that lucky.

She was twenty-one the first time she tried to go home again, returning with a husband in a navy-blue suit and a toddler perched on her hip. They hadn't called first, and there'd been no way to prepare her parents. Barbara's father had been easier to win over. When he opened the door, Billy grinned and reached for him. Acting on instinct, perhaps seeing something familiar in the little boy's face, her father didn't stand a chance. He reached back.

Not Barbara's mother, though. She hadn't touched her grandson the first day, as he sat on the floor with his grandfather, both making *vroom vroom* noises with Billy's small collection of Matchbox cars.

Years later, the threat to disown her after the divorce was similarly vanquished. This time, the twins were a help. Billy was starting his teen years without a male role model. The assumption was Barbara had left Ohio to live closer to her parents. A divorcee with three children and a high school education, she would need all the help she could get. How could they refuse?

A year later, when it became clear Barbara had returned to the east coast, not to her parents, but for a man, the disowning was easier to accomplish. First, her father died. Then, her mother severed all ties.

Billy's high school graduation forced Barbara to let her mother back into her life. She wrote a letter. Well, perhaps that's overstating. She mailed an invitation to the graduation party and signed her name. It reminded her of the time seventeen years before, when she had sent a birth announcement. Her mother left her RSVP on the answering machine, betraying no emotion. On the day of the barbeque, Barbara introduced her to the guests with the same forced politeness. They spent the afternoon on opposite sides of the backyard, exactly how they got through the next thirty years.

The only reason Barbara made attempts to salvage a relationship with her mother was for the benefit of the children. Over the years, she has had many opportunities to doubt the wisdom of this decision.

***

Oliver is curled up on the bed when she returns, sleeping, as if he didn't notice she was gone. Barbara slides under the covers, trying not to wake him. He's a gray shorthair, fifteen years old, and he's developed some crotchety behavior lately, including a new, high-pitched yowl Barbara can't decipher as pain or confusion or random complaint. She's taken him to the vet and been told the obvious: he's getting old. Whether arthritis or dementia, all she knows for sure is how irritating it is. She doesn't dare reach out to stroke his soft fur, instead watches his back rise and fall, lulling her to sleep. She tossed and turned at her mother's house the night before.

She wakes after dark, disoriented. Letting herself fall asleep so late in the day had been a bad idea.

She shuffles down the hall to the kitchen. The freezer is stocked with dinners for one. It reminds her of a joke Bill used to tell. She can only remember the punchline. *Because you're ugly*. The girls would moan and roll their eyes at every retelling. How does it start? Barbara yawns and reaches for the orange chicken with rice.

She's stabbing the cellophane with a fork when a realization hits—her mother is dead. Not that she'd forgotten, exactly. Maybe it's the thought of Bill. Dead, too. Maybe they're together, shooting the breeze. Barbara isn't sure she believes in any of that. It's probably nothing more than a comforting tale parents tell their children because they can't bear to admit their own uncertainty.

Barbara doesn't go to church anymore, but she'd been raised Catholic. Her father was a deacon in the church. She received all the sacraments and felt perverse giddiness when she made her first confession, spinning an elaborate lie about stealing her mother's brooch. She was eight by then and already had genuine sins to confess, but they weren't any of the priest's business.

It's easy to become lost in memories, now when there's more life behind her than ahead.

Barbara pours herself a glass of water and sets the hot plastic tray on a towel to carry it into the den. There, she sits in Bill's recliner—it will always be his—and snaps on the television, drowning out her own thoughts.

***

From a distance, Barbara watches as Jenna pushes Ruby on the swings. She waves to her granddaughter, who is insistent on being watched. Is this a phase? Barbara can't remember her own children going through it. Perhaps it's a sign of the times, all these young people sending each other photos of their food, demanding attention for every little thing. It can't be healthy. Still, she waves. This is what being a grandparent requires; it isn't her job to worry. Not her job, not her place. No control over anything.

She sees Stewart before he sees her. He's following a little poodle around, the red leash slack in his right hand, a rolled-up magazine in his left. He's wearing khaki shorts and sandals with socks. And a ridiculous floppy hat. Out of the corner of her eye, she can tell he's seen her, and she expects him to turn around. Instead, to Barbara's horror, he walks right to her.

"I was thinking about you, and here you are."

Barbara looks up, startled although she'd seen him coming. "Thinking of me?"

"Yes, I feel I owe you an apology for the way I left the other night."

Barbara feels the heat rising to her cheeks. Was that only a few nights ago? "Oh, there's no need to apologize."

"I'd like to." Stewart sits on the bench next to her, though she did not invite him. The little dog sits at his feet. He leans close and lowers his voice. "I was overwhelmed, I think, and I didn't know how to behave. It's not a situation I often find myself in."

Barbara smiles. "No?"

Stewart shakes his head. "And I'm afraid I behaved quite ungentlemanly. I kicked myself the whole way home. I should have asked if I could see you again."

"Oh, that's all right," she says. She notices how pale his calves are, for the end of summer. How often does he wear these shorts? She bends to scratch the dog's head.

"This is Trudy. She was really my wife's dog, but we get on okay. Right, Trudy?" He ruffles the poodle's curls somewhat roughly, but the dog leans in, closing her eyes.

"I'd probably be more of a German Shepherd guy, or Saint Bernard, maybe, if I had my druthers. How about you?"

"Hm?"

"Are you a dog person?"

Barbara has always thought this was a bizarre expression. She does not consider herself a dog person, a cat person, a kid person, or a people person. She has deeply loved individual members of each group but can make no such sweeping claim. It's strictly case by case. "I have a cat," she says. "Oliver. I like dogs, but my job involved a lot of travel, so." She shrugs. "Cats are less needy."

Stewart nods. "Trudy's quite the diva."

Barbara laughs, regarding the fluffy white ball at their feet.

"So waddyasay?" Stewart turns to her. "Can I see you again?"

Before she can answer, Ruby charges over. "You weren't watching!" she accuses, hands on her hips. Then she sees the dog, and all's forgiven. She sits in the grass as Jenna catches up, scolding her for running off.

Barbara does the introductions, getting to Stewart last. "We're in book club together," she lies. "We recently read 1984."

"I've always wanted to join a book club," Jenna says.

"Can I take the doggy for a walk?" Ruby's pulling the leash from Stewart, and Jenna's telling her to be polite, apologizing for her as she pries Ruby's hands free.

"Oh, it's really fine," Stewart says. "I'm sure Trudy would love a wander, and she's much too elderly to pull Ruby over, if you're worried."

"That's nice of you," Jenna says. "Ruby, thank Mr. Talbot for letting us borrow Trudy for a walk."

"Thank you!" Ruby jumps in the air and Barbara wonders if she has too much energy for the poor dog, but as she and Jenna walk away, they keep a reasonable pace.

"Book club?"

"Should I have told her we met online and had sex in her childhood bedroom the first night we met?"

"I guess I assumed you'd leave the last part out."

Barbara notices the magazine unfurled on the bench beside him. *Rolling Stone,* with a certain, late-night host on the cover.

"What if she'd asked me about the book?"

"Hasn't everyone read *1984*?"

"A hundred years ago!"

"No one reads the book in book club. It's an excuse to drink wine and socialize."

Stewart narrows his eyes at her. "Are you even *in* a book club?"

Barbara shrugs. "I've thought about joining one."

Stewart slaps his thigh as he laughs, shakes his head. Before Jenna and Ruby return, she agrees to meet him for dinner on Friday.

***

On the walk to the car, Ruby holds each of their hands. "One, two, three, wheel!" she prompts, picking up her feet so they'll swing her. Barbara starts to oblige, but Jenna acts like Ruby is a dead weight.

"Mommy's tired, kiddo," Jenna says, and Ruby doesn't launch so much as the beginning of a whine.

Barbara sends a sideways glance over Ruby's head, but Jenna refuses to catch it. During the drive back, Jenna reveals her mother's funeral will be on Saturday.

"I'll go up the night before and stay at the house, and Sam will drive the kids up in the morning. You're welcome to ride up with either of us." They pass Creamy Town, and Barbara watches in the rearview mirror as Ruby's wide blue eyes follow the sign.

"It's better if I have my own car." As much as Barbara might enjoy a slumber party with her daughters, she has no desire to share in a prolonged goodbye. The grandmother they mourn was not the same woman Barbara had known.

"If you're sure."

Barbara nods, and the subject is dropped.

Ruby's *Frozen* soundtrack ends, and Jenna switches to the radio for the rest of the drive.

Barbara's car is in the driveway, and usually she'd leave from here, but today she pretends to need the bathroom. Ruby heads for the living room couch, excited for the half hour of cartoons she's allowed to watch while Jenna gets dinner ready.

Barbara opens the medicine cabinet over the sink, not sure what she's looking for, but sure she won't find it in the guest bathroom. Barbara is hardwired to recognize deception, and something doesn't add up. She has a queasy feeling in her stomach that reminds her of the summer eight years ago when they told her about Sam's cancer. Barbara had known for days something was wrong, but they hadn't told her until the day before his surgery. He'd done chemo and radiation, which killed his sperm. He's fine now, unless he's not. Unless it's back.

Barbara paces in the tiny room, hating the layout of every hall bath ever fitted into a modest house. Sink, toilet, tub. Not enough space for two people to use the sink. No closet for keeping extra towels.

Barbara hears metal pots crashing together in the kitchen. What if it's Jenna who's sick?

She exits the bathroom and in the living room, Ruby is slack-jawed and glassy-eyed. Jenna's filling a pot at the kitchen sink. Barbara corners her daughter, keeping her voice lower than the volume on the television. "Tell me," she says.

Jenna rolls her eyes, unimpressed by her mother's theatrics.

"Why is Ruby on her best behavior? She didn't bug you to stop for ice cream on the way home."

"Ruby's a good kid." She shrugs, reading the back of a pasta box as if she doesn't know it will take eight minutes to cook.

"You said you were tired. You were huffing and puffing at the park. Why are you so tired?"

Jenna takes a deep breath and seems to consider whether to make something up. In the end, she must be too tired for that, too. She closes her eyes and exhales. "I'm pregnant."

Barbara gasps. She's relieved and excited, but also confused. Ruby was a miracle of science, conceived with hormone shots and donor sperm. Over a year of effort and more money than Jenna would ever reveal, but she swore she'd never put herself through it again.

"But how?"

"I did in-vitro again. This time, it worked on the first try."

"Did you get Liam's help again?" Liam is Jenna's gay best friend, Ruby's biological father. Jenna doesn't believe in lying to children, and it's all out in the open, to Barbara's complete bewilderment.

"Yes, Mom. Liam again." She reaches out to catch her mother's hands which, Barbara now realizes, have been clutched to her chest. "But it's different this time."

"Different?"

"The baby isn't mine."

"What?"

"I'm having this baby for Liam. Liam and Marco."

"*What?*"

"Liam will raise the baby with his husband. We'll be part of the family the way Liam is part of ours now, with Ruby.

Suddenly, the room seems too bright, and Barbara winces, unable to catch her breath or speak. She thinks she might be having a stroke. She lets Jenna lead her to a chair at the kitchen table. "No, no, no, no." It's all she can manage.

"I know this isn't exactly conventional." Jenna moves back to the stove, throws the pasta in the pot of boiling water, and turns down the burner.

"Conventional?" Barbara chokes. "This is insane. Does Sam know?"

"Of course." Jenna laughs. "Everyone knows."

"Will and Ruby?"

Jenna sits at the table, nodding. "It's important for everyone to understand what's going on."

"You think Ruby understands this?"

"I do."

"She understands you're *giving away* her full sibling?"

"It's not as if we're abandoning him on a random doorstep."

"Him?" Barbara blinks. "How pregnant are you?"

Jenna shakes her head. "I was being hypothetical. It's too early to know."

"When are you due?"

"May."

Barbara does the counting in her head. "I still have time to talk you out of it."

Jenna sighs. "You won't be able to." She maintains eye contact as she speaks. "This isn't something we jumped into. We've been discussing this for a long time. Years."

Liam and Marco had gotten married as soon as it became legal in New Hampshire, seven or eight years before. They'd moved closer when Ruby was born. Barbara loved them. They were like family. *Like* family.

"This is my grandbaby we're talking about. I will not let you—"

"Let me?" Jenna lifts her eyebrows.

Barbara takes a breath and holds it. Counts to ten. "I know you, Jenna. You're not capable of this."

"I don't imagine it's going to be easy. I'm sure there are times now when it's hard for Liam. He gave us an amazing gift with Ruby, and now I'm in the position to return the favor."

"Favor!" Barbara scoffs. "It's a baby, not a ride to the airport!"

"I'm completely aware it's a baby. Ruby was a baby too."

Barbara shakes her head. "It's different for a mother."

Jenna leans back in her chair. "Do you really believe that? I'm surprised."

"Surprised?"

"You feel like you were closer to us than Bill was?"

Precarious territory. For most of their lives, the twins had believed he was their stepfather. The truth was too complicated. They were four years old before Barbara had been able to leave her first husband. Their paternity didn't seem relevant at the time. It had been exposed eventually, though Barbara never thought the distinction should matter.

"Aren't you the one who thinks biology is so important?" Barbara asks.

"Not biology, no. Honesty." Jenna's jaw clenches, and she breathes through her nose. "I think children should be able to trust the adults in their lives. I can't believe, after all these years, you still don't understand." She stands and switches off the burner. "You should go. Sam will be home soon. He'll invite you to stay and I—" She rifles through a drawer for a plastic spoon, slams it. "You should go." She's usually calm. This must be the hormones.

Barbara stands but pauses by the door. "Did your grandmother know you were planning this?"

"We'd talked about it."

Of all the things to be concerned about, this shouldn't register, but it does.

"You can't sign rights away until after the birth." Barbara can't remember where she's heard this, or whether it's true.

Jenna turns back to the stove.

Chapter Three

Barbara has a full-length mirror hanging on the inside of her closet door. She rarely uses it. She looks in the mirror above the bathroom sink when she's doing her makeup, though she prefers the palm-sized rectangle compact. A glance at the larger mirror to ensure she hasn't overdone the blusher. As time marches forward, she's seen her mother in her reflection more and more. She's always hated it, but it's especially bizarre, now that her mother's *gone*.

Such a strange euphemism. Right now, Barbara knows exactly where her mother is: lying in a funeral home in Boothbay, Maine, wearing a dress her granddaughters chose for her.

Barbara sets aside three dark dresses for tomorrow: black, navy, and charcoal gray. She can decide in the morning. She probably should have canceled the date with Stewart. She thought about it several times but couldn't make herself dial his number. What if he thought she was blowing him off and didn't ask to reschedule?

She'd insist they have an early night, which would slow things down if he didn't stay over.

She decides on the teal paisley wraparound. She has beads in the exact same shade. Standing sideways in the mirror, she sucks in her stomach.

Barbara's mother had always been a round woman. Upside-down pear-shaped, she'd called it. Barbara pictures it as an egg on toothpicks. Busty with slim legs. Barbara spent most of her life fighting it, but like all family legacies, it caught up with her.

She ballooned with her first pregnancy, starved herself once Billy was born and his father made clear what was expected of her. He wouldn't take her with him when he went to church on Sunday until she was *presentable*. He acted like he was doing her a favor. She wouldn't have thought she'd care about going to church but it was her only social time in Ohio, the only time he let her talk to other adults.

She didn't gain as much weight when she was pregnant with the twins; she was sick the whole time, and then, they came early—even according to the altered due date Barbara was using.

Barbara's weight went up and down in her thirties and forties. In menopause, however, it got, well, *stuck*. Whatever fad diet she tried—no carbs, no sugar, no solid food of any kind—nothing worked. She tried a cleanse after the holidays and spent the week with a headache, snapping at people. Her hair started falling out and she didn't lose a single pound. She's trying to accept this body as a reality, to start thinking of herself as curvy. Men like their women with a little meat on them, right? Something to hold on to, a nice big booty. Well, Barbara has that.

Also, who cares what men want? She's spent a lifetime worrying about that, and what has she got to show for it?

Julie never inherited the family figure, but Jenna has always been a bit chubby, even as a kid. Sam doesn't seem to mind. He dotes on her as if she looks like Cindy

Crawford, always has. It's too early to tell with Ruby — could be baby fat.

Yesterday, she picked up Ruby from her first day of kindergarten. They stopped for ice cream on the condition it would be their secret. Jenna was a stickler about sweets. Both nights, when she brought Ruby home, she was invited for dinner, but she said she couldn't stay. Tonight, it was true.

Jenna had already left for Boothbay when Barbara dropped Ruby at home. She'd help her sister get the house for those guests who would be invited back after the funeral. Barbara isn't sure how she'll get through the day without losing her cool. Since Jenna told her about her plans for this pregnancy, Barbara has felt a combustible panic. She wants to ground her or kidnap her, but she will have to think of something less extreme. She's powerless in this world. Her grandchild can be given away and she can't do anything about it.

She's not giving up, though. She has nine months to convince Jenna to see things her way.

***

Tonight, Stewart is wearing a camel-colored suit jacket. His silver hair has been cut recently. He takes her to the new Italian place downtown, which means they must find street parking. Barbara leans forward in the passenger seat, on the lookout. He gives her credit for locating a spot only steps from the entrance and pumps his fist in the air in victory.

On their first date, they had exchanged the essential information, fleshed out the biographies from their dating profiles. Stewart is a widower of five years. Recovered alcoholic, non-smoker. He has two sons in the military. Air Force. Stewart's father was in the Air Force but apparently, it had skipped a generation. Stewart was a lawyer, retired now.

Barbara's dating profile lists her as divorced—not a lie, exactly. She has been divorced. She's never liked clicking the *widow* box, which seemed to induce pity in others. Barbara believes pity is one of those emotions that seems kind but isn't. People are most likely to feel pity when they're concerned what happened to you might happen to them. Also, pity inspires a morbid curiosity that is anything but kind. As far as she's concerned, pity is selfish and nosy.

But Stewart has been up front about his wife's death, and it makes Barbara feel sneaky. She decides to start the evening by getting this off her chest. As soon as the waitress takes their order, she folds her hands on the tablecloth in front of her and clears her throat.

Stewart gives her his full attention.

"I'm a private person, and there is one thing I leave off my profile until I decide I want to get to know someone better."

"Oh?" Stewart smiles, cautiously.

"My second husband passed away eighteen years ago. My first marriage was brief and ended in divorce. It's easier to mention this in—" She pauses, pretending to struggle for the words she's rehearsed. "Introductory interactions."

"I see." Stewart scowls at the tabletop as he seems to process this. "I suppose there is some stigma to widowhood, isn't there?"

Barbara sighs, relieved. "Oh, yes. I think so."

"How did your husband die?" he ventures. "If I'm not prying."

"Oh, heart failure. He was sick for a long time before he passed."

Stewart reaches across the table and places his hand on top of hers. "I'm sorry."

"It's all right." She doesn't talk about it much and is surprised to find herself getting misty. She blinks it away. "This was a long time ago."

"But sometimes it feels fresh." He takes his hand back. "I understand."

"Of course, you do." Barbara busies herself unwrapping her silverware from the cloth napkin. "How did your wife pass?"

"Breast cancer."

She shakes her head. "How old were your boys?"

"They'd already left home. What about you?"

"Almost. My oldest was away in med school. The girls were home still. Jenna came back from college to help."

"Jenna's the one I met at the park the other day?"

"Yes."

"With little Ruby."

Barbara smiles. "Don't let her hear you call her little. Her older brother's eleven and she's desperate to catch up."

Stewart chuckles. "Oh, I remember. I had an older brother. He was *so* cool."

The servers come with the food then. His is manicotti; she ordered the risotto.

"Do you have siblings?" he asks when they're alone again.

Barbara shakes her head and answers quickly. "I was an only child." She's said this so often it doesn't feel untrue anymore.

"Are your parents still around?"

"Well, my father's been gone for years, but—" This time, the pause is not rehearsed. "Actually, my mother's funeral is tomorrow."

He sets down his fork. "Oh, god. Tomorrow?"

She shrugs.

"I'm sorry."

"It's fine. We weren't close."'

"Well, I'm sorry about that, too." He offers a glum smile.

Barbara insists he continue eating and takes a big bite of risotto to encourage him. Somehow, this adds to the uncomfortable lull. She swallows, reaches for her water. "How about you? Your parents?"

"Believe it or not, my dad's still around. Just turned ninety. We've gotten to be good buddies the last few years."

"That's nice." She's grateful they've managed to sidestep to a less depressing subject. "Does he live in town?"

Stewart nods, his mouth full. They move on to brag about their grandchildren, much safer territory. They take out their phones and show photos. When they've finished their meals, they agree to split a tiramisu. Stewart waits for her to take the first bite, then follows with a forkful of the exact same size.

When they're leaving, he helps with her coat. He stands behind her as she fastens the buttons, and his firm grip on her upper arms makes her wish she didn't have an early morning. He keeps a hand lightly on her back as they walk to the car and she gets in first. In her driveway, they make out like teenagers. Later, after she manages to put herself to bed, alone, she's suddenly worried about what her neighbors have seen.

It's still dark outside when Barbara leaves in the morning. She has the queasy, disoriented feeling she associates with all those pre-dawn flights for business trips. The rush to get there on time, the feeling of being important, in demand, needed. There was nothing else with that feeling, not even motherhood. The girls were in high school by then, and they had each other or Bill. Nothing she could do at home couldn't be done as well by someone else—helping with homework or making brownies or loading a dishwasher. But the success of the business depended on her and her alone. There was no one else who knew the answer or could do the presentation. When she was home, she answered calls during dinner and wrote emails after everyone else in the house was asleep. She was a job creator. The decisions she made mattered.

It already feels like another life.

Of course, it's possible she'd been fooling herself all along. After she sold the company, no one called her to help them figure things out. They found someone else to do what she'd done all those years. Apparently, she wasn't as irreplaceable as she thought.

There are few cars on the road at this hour, and she wonders about their plans in a way she never would during daylight hours. The only places open this early are airports and hospitals.

Today will mark the final Catholic sacrament of her mother's life. Barbara's father taught her Catholic funerals were different from other Christian funerals, not intended to celebrate the life of the deceased or provide closure for their families. While Protestants and Presbyterians were assured that Jesus died for their sins so they might enjoy everlasting life, Catholics were never provided such an unconditional guaranty. He made every other kind of Christian sound childish and naïve. What made Catholics more mature, and therefore superior, was their belief in purgatory, an in-between state of nothingness where the soul was at risk of getting trapped indefinitely. The Catholic funeral fulfilled a very practical purpose of conveying the soul to Heaven based upon the prayers of those who loved them.

Barbara isn't sure she believes in God, but she can't shake the feeling this day is meant to ensure her mother's soul doesn't get stuck on its way back to her father. She refuses to be held responsible for that, too.

The highway fills in as she's looking for her exit ramp.

Jenna says the concept of purgatory is old-school, but Barbara knows her mother was old-school. About church and marriage and babies. There's no way she would have approved of this nonsense of Jenna's, giving away her child.

The church parking lot is nearly full, making Barbara feel oddly proud. People are getting out of their cars, elderly couples and families dressed in black. It's been so long since she lived here, and the only person she recognizes is the friend Julie calls Hooley—Michael Houlihan. They dated once, a million years ago. At the time, Barbara thought they might get married. Julie fell apart after their breakup and moved home for a while. Of course, Barbara hated seeing her daughter torn up, but it was nice to be her safe place for once

Hooley's leaning against a beat-up, red truck, smoking a cigarette. He looks like he's in no rush to get inside. Barbara understands the feeling.

***

Our Lady Queen of Peace is on the water, with its wooden rafters and high, curved ceiling resembling a ship's hull turned upside down. The large upstairs sanctuary will be open until Columbus Day, when all the summer people have gone home and the year-round congregants move to the small chapel downstairs with low ceilings, easier to heat. Barbara's family attended services here for as long as she can remember. When she was ten, President John F. Kennedy had visited with his sister. The priests kept the visit from Secret Service under wraps, and no one had known he was coming, and her mother missed the whole thing. Those were the years when she wasn't getting out of bed before noon.

Today, Barbara sits in the front pew between Jenna and Julie. The wake was the night before. She doesn't mind having missed the up-close view of her mother lying dead at the front of the room. Now the casket is closed, draped in white cloth. The priest standing at the altar looks to be about sixteen years old. She imagines his robes are merely a costume concealing jeans and a sports jersey.

Barbara knows it's none of her business, but Ruby's wearing pants, which might explain why she found it acceptable to run around the church with some older boys before the service. Now, she has grass stains on her knees and a new scab forming on her chin.

Barbara never brought her children to funerals. That's what babysitters are for. When her father died, she'd come alone, skipped the church and showed up to the graveside. Her mother had not looked at her, had not spoken to her, had not invited her back to the house. Barbara had driven three hours to stare at the hole they'd dug for her father, and then she drove three hours back. When Bill asked how it was, she simply said: "Over."

At the cemetery, Barbara sees his gravestone for the first time. *Loving husband and father*. He'd been buried on a warm and sunny day, nothing like today's chilly damp. The memories come unbidden, and she wants none of them. A day like this is particularly treacherous.

The priest from the church service somehow has more to say. Then Jenna steps forward and tells stories about the many times in her life she turned to her grandmother for advice. Barbara thinks it sounds like she's paying tribute to the mother she never had. Ruby leans sleepily against Sam. A long day already, and not lunchtime yet.

The shiny, gray casket is lowered into the earth beside Barbara's father. Each passing moment gets checked off a mental list, the final obligations of the dutiful, disowned daughter. Her mother would have wanted to avoid the appearance of any estrangement. She throws a handful of dirt on the casket to keep strangers from being uncomfortable and to honor the wishes of a dead woman who would never be satisfied.

Everyone gets in their cars waiting to follow the girls. Barbara thinks: *Almost over.* She turns and squeezes Jenna's hand. "All right. I'll see you on Monday then."

"Aren't you coming back to the house?"

Barbara feels like she's done everything that could possibly be expected of her. She longs to curl up in bed with a cup of tea. Peel off these stupid nylons and put on her warm, baggy pajamas. "I thought I'd head home." Surely, she's made enough polite conversation with people she'll never see again in her life.

"We're going to talk about the will when everyone leaves."

"You don't need me for that."

Jenna looks puzzled. "You're in the will, Mom."

"No, I'm not." Barbara pats Jennas shoulder when she starts to protest. "It's okay. I never expected to be." She can still hear her mother making the proclamations, as if she'd cared. Like what she needed from her mother could have been quantified by a bank balance.

"No, Mom, you're in the will. I know you are. Rick's the executor. He told us last night who she named. It's only the three of us: you, me, and Julie."

So much of this is startling, she doesn't know where to start. "Not Billy?"

"I don't think they were close." Jenna shrugs. As they walk to their cars, she explains an odd, second detail. Apparently, her grandmother had chosen Rick to be the executor while he and Julie were married. The divorce was amicable, and there'd been no reason to change it.

On the drive to the house, Barbara has time to consider why her mother named her in the will. There is nothing sentimental to hope for, some emblematic object of her mother's love. It's more likely something meant to shame her in front of her own children, a way to get the final word, one last jab.

What cruel secrets were left to be exposed?

***

Barbara stands near a table with cold cuts and cheese, not wanting to make a commitment. The couch is already occupied by three white-haired women she doesn't envy. It's hard to extricate oneself from couch-level conversation. Those women may well be there in the morning.

Across the room, Jenna and Sam are talking to the priest, who has shed his robes and turns out to be dressed like an adult after all. Maybe an illusion, but Barbara thinks she can see the beginnings of a baby bump beneath the black fabric of Jenna's funeral dress. Ruby and Will are nowhere in sight and have probably disappeared to play on the beach. Ruby won't even need to change.

Barbara finds herself nodding at the meaningless platitudes of people who, for all she knows, knew her mother better than she did—which isn't saying much.

Her mother had been a widow for thirty-four years. Compared to that, what's eighteen? The two women had so much in common—early widowhood and difficult relationships with their children. They might have had a lot to talk about if they'd ever tried.

After approximately half an hour, Barbara gives herself permission to hide in the kitchen. Unfortunately, she finds more people there, crowded around the coffee maker. This house is much smaller than anywhere else she's ever lived. Even the house she'd rented on Essex Street as a single mother had a pantry and a second bathroom. There is nowhere to escape to.

Julie comes in with a stack of dirty plates to set in the sink. Her long hair is pulled into a loose braid that's come looser since this morning. Barbara wants to pull her aside to ask how she's doing. They've barely had a chance to exchange more than several sentences all day.

"You remember Mrs. McClure," Julie says helpfully before being pulled away again. Barbara turns to the woman on her left. Mrs. McClure has shriveled up since she last saw her, forty years ago. That summer, the McClures went on a cruise, and Barbara watered their plants while they were away. She'd spent hours lying in the woman's brass bed with Bill, the ideal rendezvous point for a couple of philanderers, each staying with their parents for the summer. By then, they'd already exhausted boat shacks and sand dunes. It was hard to cuddle in a tool shed. Next door, her father recovered from his first heart attack; her mother grew increasingly frustrated at Barbara's insistence on staying in Maine so long. Her father didn't need two people caring for him. Weeks had passed. He was ready to start working half-days back at the office.

Mrs. McClure leans in and asks about the weather in Ohio, and Barbara thinks, *Of course*. That's what her mother had told people to explain why they never saw her only daughter. She had lived in Ohio for a while, that wasn't far from the truth. It was the kind of lie Barbara would tell.

She remembers her mother standing in the doorway of Mrs. McClure's bedroom. She'd never heard her footsteps on the stairs or in the hallway. Neither of them had, consumed by their lovemaking.

Her mother's voice was flat. "Your husband's on the phone." They pulled apart, tried to cover their nakedness. But there was no way to feign innocence. Her mother continued: "He's with Billy in the ER."

Barbara's emotions went from her deepest shame to her deepest terror. She threw on her clothing and ran home, without looking back, without saying goodbye.

Only a broken arm, but enough to send her back to Ohio.

"Rainy and cold," Barbara tells Mrs. McClure.

She didn't see Bill again until the day the girls were born.

At the first pause in conversation, she excuses herself and goes upstairs. In her mother's room, she finds Ruby asleep on the bed. The nap looks surreptitious; she hasn't removed her shoes or burrowed beneath the covers. Perhaps, sleep came upon her before she knew what was happening. That's how it is with children. Barbara remembers once coming upon a younger Jenna asleep in a corner of the house during her own birthday party. She finds a spare blanket to spread across her granddaughter and climbs in beside her, making spoons.

***

"Mom?"

When Barbara wakes, Ruby's gone. Jenna's sitting at the foot of the bed.

"Mostly everyone left. It's safe to come back down." She forces a smile. "I know this has all been hard on you."

Barbara sits up and runs a hand through her hair. There's so much they can't talk about. She can't articulate any of what she really feels: resentment, ambivalence, relief. "I'm fine, dear. How are you?"

"First trimester fatigue." She sighs. "You know, my doctor called it a geriatric pregnancy."

Barbara doesn't trust herself here either. She wants to get through this day without an explosion. She decides to keep things light. "Ouch."

Jenna nods. "Okay." She gets to her feet. "Rick's getting things ready in the living room. I'm making coffee. Want one?"

"Sure."

When Barbara enters the room, seats have already been chosen. The girls are on the couch. Rick is in the wingback. Sam is in the kitchen with the children.

They've left her the pale blue recliner, her mother's chair. Her coffee waits on the end table.

"Well, I know the coffee table's mine." Jenna slides her fingers under the table and retrieves a circular orange sticker. "Grammy made me go through her things eons ago. I was living with Liam, and we didn't have any real furniture. I picked stuff for you too," she tells Julie. "Your stickers are pink."

Julie stands and begins feeling the undersides of various things in the room. She finds a pink sticker on the cuckoo clock. "Of course," she says, laughing. And then the laughing is crying.

Jenna stands and hugs her, and they cry together for several long moments. Barbara sips her coffee. The caffeine will help her stay awake on the trip home.

The girls return to their seats.

"I can't believe she's gone," Julie says.

Jenna nods. "We're lucky we had her for this long."

Barbara's mother once dragged her into the bathroom by her hair, shoving a bar of soap into her mouth hard enough to dislodge a tooth. She reminds herself for the hundredth time her daughters are not grieving for the same person. Barbara looks out the window. She hates driving after dark.

"The will isn't incredibly detailed," Rick begins. "But she left the house to both of you and some money in an account to help with taxes if you don't want to sell."

"Do you want to sell?" Julie asks Jenna.

Jenna shakes her head. "You live here."

They bicker politely over this. Jenna says she doesn't need the money, and she looks forward to more family beach vacations. Rick suggests he and Julie could buy her out at some point. Julie looks surprised by this, and he stresses that he's talking about their reno business. It would be a good investment. They should renovate before putting it on the market. They all agree they don't need to make any decision now. Barbara does not weigh in.

Then there are boxes to distribute. Unfortunately, Rick does this one at a time; Barbara is unable to open hers while the girls are distracted with theirs.

Jenna's box contains her grandmother's wedding band and engagement ring. It's a simple setting, in gold, nothing like more modern ring sets. But it's a half-karat diamond she could always have reset for Will or Ruby in the future. Though, Barbara wonders whether people will still be getting married by then. When Jenna took Sam's last name fifteen years ago, it already seemed old-fashioned. Julie's box contains a strand of pearls. Apparently, there's a familiar story Barbara has never heard. They were an anniversary gift from Barbara's father, for their twenty-fifth year of marriage. These are the only pieces of jewelry he ever bought for her, and the only ones she wore.

Barbara's box is bigger than the other two. She takes it from Rick, feeling the weight. The contents could be a table lamp, a Keurig, or a vase. Her pulse races, and she wracks her brain. Perhaps she should take it home unopened. This would make her daughters angry, reminding them of her secret keeping. Better to simply get it over with.

She lifts the cover off and lets it fall to the floor as soon as she sees what's inside: an urn. The pottery is a simple shape, painted blue. There's only one person whose ashes could be inside, but to remove any doubt, the name is engraved at the bottom.

"Who's James?" Julie asks. She's standing up, leaning forward and craning her neck to read upside down.

Suddenly, Barbara's eyes are wet; her mouth is dry.

"There's a note," Jenna says, bending to retrieve the lid, which has an envelope taped to the inside. She holds it out to her mother.

Barbara reaches with trembling fingers.

The envelope is blank, but Barbara tears it open to delay having to speak. She can't. She lets herself hope there will be some explanation, knowing better. There is no note. Inside the envelope, there are three photographs.

In the first, James is in a hospital bassinette; his eyes are shut, and there's a cap on his head pulled low, making him look like any other baby.

In the second, Barbara sees herself at five, propped up on the sofa, a pillow under her elbow to help support the baby's head. She wasn't allowed to pick him up or carry him. If she wanted to hold him, she had to sit like this.

It must have been the day he came home from the hospital. The photo is black and white, but she sees the blue of his sailor suit, the pale yellow of her dress. She never thought she'd see his face again.

"Mom?"

"She told me she'd thrown them all away," she whispers. It was probably the best way her mother knew to end the conversation, to keep Barbara from looking for them. She still remembers the day she came home from school and found them all gone. If she'd known ahead of time, she would have hidden them away. If only she could have kept one to press within the pages of her diary. Probably this one.

"Who?" Jenna asks.

The third photo is of James as a toddler on the beach. He's holding a plastic shovel and grinning. The waves behind him make Barbara's stomach churn.

She places the photos in the box and takes the lid from Jenna. "Leave it to my mother," Barbara says, almost to herself. She struggles to close the box, pinching the corners. Always easier for things to spill out than to shove them back inside.

Jenna sits on her coffee table and reaches to still Barbara's hands. She's close; their knees are touching. Julie's still standing behind her. Rick has excused himself to the kitchen.

"Talk to us," Jenna says.

Barbara doesn't look up. She keeps her eyes on the box; her hands are on either side, with Jenna's hands on her wrists.

"I never knew they had him cremated." Keeping cremains was not old-school Catholic, not at all. Barbara wonders if her father had known.

Jenna tightens her grasp. "James."

Barbara nods. "My brother."

"When did he die?"

"He was three." Barbara was only eight. Still old enough to be responsible.

Jenna gasps. "Oh, Mom. I'm sorry."

"How did we never know you had a brother?" Julie demands.

"We were never to speak of it." And they never had, as if he'd never existed.

Julie sits on the table beside her sister. Her voice softens. "How did he die?"

"Drowned."

Jenna starts crying then, and Julie turns to her, perplexed. Jenna's not a crier.

"I'm sorry. It's the hormones. It's so terrible."

Barbara sighs. "Yes, it's terrible." She pulls her hands free and gets to her feet. She hugs the box to her chest. "I need to go home."

"Now?"

"It's been a long day."

Chapter Four

When Barbara gets home, she puts the ashes on the kitchen table and crawls into bed without undressing, except for the nylons. She'd had to fight to stay awake the whole drive back, but now she can't get to sleep. Near dawn, she moves to the den and watches infomercials from Bill's chair. She hasn't upgraded the cable since her retirement. She was never home enough to justify anything beyond the basic package that includes internet. Jenna has all the channels and can scroll forever before getting back where she started.

Tonight, she's longing for the History Channel or a wildlife documentary. Even cartoons. Instead, she watches about absorbent cloths, food processors, car wax. Something more distracting would keep her from having to think about it. About what to do with the ashes. She can't keep them. After all these years, knowing they're in the house—it's all she can think about. In movies, people are always scattering ashes at the beach. The thought sends a shiver down her spine.

Her mother blamed her. She'd only been eight. Barbara blamed herself. Old enough to pay attention.

A baby can drown in two inches of standing water. She remembers a nurse telling her this in the hospital after Billy was born, a caution about bath time she already knew.

Maybe she could bury them at her parents' grave. There are probably rules; she'd have to ask the priest's permission, that young boy who never knew her brother had ever existed. She rubs her temples as she imagines explaining. Could she write it in a letter? Maybe she could plant a lilac bush. Dig a very deep hole. Tell no one.

This was the lesson of her childhood. After James died, her mother had spent time in a mental hospital. When she returned home, they weren't to speak about any of it. Everything went back to normal, except James was gone. And Barbara's mother no longer accompanied them to Sunday mass. Did losing a child cause a crisis in faith? Barbara honored the family code of silence and never asked.

Too late to ask now.

Eventually, Oliver locates her, jumps up onto her lap, and does a demonstration of the very thing that eludes her.

***

The urn sits on the kitchen table all weekend. Jenna's left several messages; Barbara only texts back to keep her from dropping by.

I'm fine. Talk Monday.

She sleeps most of Sunday and is grateful the grocery store is open on Labor Day. She transfers the plastic tubs of potato and mac salad into her two big, yellow serving bowls, covers them with Saran wrap, and carries them to the car. It reminds her of lugging the twins around when they were infants. They didn't like to be carried separately. She never knew if this was out of jealousy or fondness for each other. They had spent the first three months of their lives sleeping in the same incubator and developed their own gibberish language to communicate their toddler secrets.

Those months when the twins were in the hospital, she was allowed to drive to visit them. She took her husband to work in the morning and had to be home in time to meet her son after school. This period was the most freedom she'd ever known in Ohio.

It's a short drive to Jenna's house, over the bridge and past the cemetery where Bill's buried. It's the kind of drive she's done many times, no longer requiring conscious awareness. She thinks about the day Bill sneaked into the hospital and held the babies. He begged her to let him take them all away, promised to be a father to her young son. She cried and cried, but it felt impossible. How could she tell her husband she'd been unfaithful? She'd been born again by then, in a revival tent, only months after she returned from Boothbay. It was important to her at the time, this idea of a clean slate, her past forgiven, erased. She was done sinning.

Also, by then, she'd had time to doubt they'd ever really loved each other. She'd been running from a union more stifling than the childhood it had been meant to save her from. Bill had already been on his second marriage when they'd met—he was probably a playboy. And even if he thought his love was real, she couldn't trust it. Only a matter of time before he figured out what was wrong with her, like everyone else did eventually.

Barbara parks on the street, not wanting to block the cars in the driveway.

She manages to open the screen door with her arms full and finds Jenna in the kitchen, who hurries over to grab one of the bowls.

"Ooh, is that paprika?" Jenna says, peering into the bowl.

"Mmhmm," Barbara answers, because Jenna seems to think it's a good thing. Jenna's Labor Day party was an annual affair, and Barbara was not known for cooking. She was known for working, for being busy. But this was the first year since retirement.

"Looks great." Jenna finds room for them in the refrigerator and turns back with a concerned face. "How are you *doing*?" She draws out the last word meaningfully.

"Fine, fine." Barbara looks around the room. "Where are my grandbabies?"

"Will's outside helping Sam put out chairs and Ruby's upstairs getting ready."

"Getting ready?"

Jenna shrugs. "Yeah, I don't know. It seemed like there was some kind of surprise. Maybe she's dressing up the dog." She drags a chair from the table and sits down. "I thought about skipping the party this year, but the kids were looking forward to it. It's like the last hurrah of the summer."

Barbara hangs her purse on a hook by the door and sits down at the table across from her daughter. She can see into the living room and out the glass sliders where Sam and Will are pulling a plastic tablecloth across the picnic table. "Is Julie coming?"

Jenna nods. "I expect she'll get here about the time we're turning the grill on." She reaches out and touches Barbara's hand lightly with her fingertips. "I've been worried about you since Boothbay."

"I'm fine," Barbara says again as she pulls her hand away. She's always uncomfortable with how direct Jenna is, how ready she is to talk about *feelings*. She probably learned something in all those college psychology courses. It certainly hadn't come from home. "I think I'll go see what's going on with Ruby."

***

The door isn't latched, and when Barbara knocks, it swings open. Ruby's sitting cross-legged in the middle of her bed, wearing a sleeveless blue sundress, a pile of ribbons in her lap. She looks up and grins as Barbara comes in. "Nono!"

Nono. That's her name. It started with Will. Barbara had planned to have him call her Nana, but he'd had trouble with the pronunciation. Jenna liked to tell people he'd been mimicking the words he heard most often from his grandmother. It's true he'd been an extremely active infant. Barbara didn't believe in childproofing. Wrapping your kid in bubble wrap wouldn't prepare them for the real world. You must teach them about boundaries, make them learn not to touch breakables. That's what Barbara did when her kids were little. Somehow, over the years, she managed to collect more expensive breakables.

"Whatcha doin'?" Barbara sits on the edge of the bed.

"Picking a ribbon to go with my dress." She holds up the two finalists. One is red, white, and blue stripes; one is blue and purple stars.

Barbara points to the latter.

"Do you know how to do braids?"

"Not really." Barbara tries to make up for this deficiency by taking the ribbon from her granddaughter and tying it around her ponytail. "I can make a nice bow, though. Did you do your hair all by yourself?"

Ruby nods, proud. It's only slightly crooked. Barbara stands over her and tries to make the bow off-center to compensate.

"What do you think about Mom having a baby?"

"It's not our baby. It's Uncle Liam's baby."

Barbara sits back down on the edge of the bed. "Does that make you sad?"

"Why would I be sad?" Ruby's little elfin face is stricken with worry. "Uncle Liam's nice. Don't you like Uncle Liam?"

"Of course, I do. I love Liam." It's not a lie. He'd been a special part of the family for years before he gave them Ruby, and gratitude had crystalized the affection.

Ruby's baby wrinkles smooth out, leaving no trace. "He's like my other dad, you know."

Barbara grinds her teeth, but she manages to smile and nod. She'll never understand why Jenna insists on telling the kids everything. She thinks secrets are unhealthy, but not all truths are age appropriate.

"But the baby won't live here. You know that, right?"

Ruby nods.

"And that's okay with you?"

Ruby squints up at her like this is a strange question. "My friend Nicky got a baby sister over the summer, and he says she cries a lot and wakes him up at night."

Barbara sighs. She knows she shouldn't be talking Ruby into being upset if she isn't. She can't help wishing she had someone else on her side, even a five-year-old.

***

The thermometer outside says ninety-four degrees. Barbara takes a seat in the shade, which does nothing to mitigate the humidity. Jenna hands out endless popsicles to the kids, sheepishly insisting to anyone in earshot they're "sugar-free," as if her parenting skills are on trial.

Liam and Marco arrive with several boxes of sparklers, an immediate hit. Ruby leaps into Liam's arms and launches into a story Barbara can't hear. Liam's always been good with children; he's a kindergarten teacher on the other side of town.

Heads together, their physical resemblance is clear. Sam and Liam look alike, and it isn't always obvious Will and Ruby have different fathers. Liam is taller, slimmer, but their coloring is similar. Sandy brown hair and light blue eyes. Barbara has seen photos of Liam as a child, freckled and pudgy the way Ruby is now. Their milky skin is more susceptible to sunburn.

People know much more about their own genetics these days, it's hard to remember what secrets were possible a generation ago. Everything has changed, of course, with everyone sending their DNA through the mail on a lark to find out what percent Irish they are, as if it matters. And now their DNA is on file forever somewhere, which can't be a good thing. Barbara will be keeping her DNA to herself.

Liam sets Ruby down and heads toward Barbara. The last time they saw each other was weeks ago at Hampton Beach before she knew about Jenna's pregnancy. She stands up to prevent him from looming over her, and this leads him to think he should hug her.

"Looks like Jenna's outdone herself again," he says, motioning to the food spread across the picnic table.

Barbara offers Marco a cheek to kiss.

"Was she always such an overachiever?"

Barbara looks from Marco to Liam, a vibration of rage hot in her chest. Still, she manages to keep her voice cool and calm. "Yes. A people pleaser. I always had to worry about her growing up. Someone taking advantage of her."

Marco blinks; Liam frowns. "Jenna mentioned you were struggling with this," he says. The sympathy in his voice makes her think she'd be capable of committing physical violence against him. Liam. The sweet kid who has been part of the family since before he was twenty.

Barbara shrugs. "Who am I to have an opinion about any of it?"

Liam looks at his feet, dismayed. "We hope you'll get used to the idea."

"Well, that's unlikely." Out of the corner of her eye, she sees Jenna alerted to their conversation, heading over. "If you'll excuse me." Barbara pushes past them, yanks open the slider, and escapes into the air conditioning before she can be accused of making a scene. She leans against the kitchen counter for a count of three before taking a deep breath, grabbing her purse from the hook by the door, and walking out the front of the house.

Julie is in the driveway, and Barbara halts on the way to her car. "Talk some sense into your sister, will you?"

Julie's hands are free, having arrived at the party with nothing. She smiles, clueless. "What?"

"I need your help!" Barbara is shaking. "She's lost her damn mind! Can't you do *something*? For once?"

Julie's mouth sets in a straight line. She walks toward Barbara and grabs her arm. "Mom, you need to get on board if you want to be part of their lives."

Barbara snatches her arm free and walks the rest of the way to her car. She starts the engine, never thinking about Ruby or Will, who might wonder where she went without saying goodbye. She blows through a stop sign as she cranks up the AC, the blaring horn of the other driver barely registering. She knows Julie's right, of course. But being forced to realization is what makes her angriest.

***

On Tuesday, Barbara parks and walks to the gym door where the parents are lining up. At noon, a teacher comes out with a clipboard listing each kid and their "Pick-up Plan." She must show her ID before Ruby is allowed to come outside and leave with her. It's the same as last week, but it's still startlingly intense. Has the world really become much more dangerous since she was a parent? The system has changed since the last time she picked up Will a few years before. Ruby comes bouncing out the door with her comically humongous backpack. When she sees Barbara, she grins and rushes toward her. "Nono!"

Some of the parents turn, mildly perplexed.

Ruby climbs into the backseat and humors her grandmother, who thinks she can't fasten her own seatbelt.

"Tell me about your teacher," Barbara says as she starts the car.

"Miss Lynn."

"What is she like?"

"She has yellow hair like my friend Taylor. And today she had pink nail polish. I'm not allowed to wear nail polish out of the house. It's only for dress ups."

"Uh huh." Barbara looks at her own nails as she grips the steering wheel: bare, bitten down to nubs.

"My favorite polish is the glitter one. Mama says maybe in third grade. She says she doesn't want me to grow up to think I have to look fancy all the time. Is this what you think?"

Barbara feels the weight of Ruby's inquisitive scowl in the rear-view mirror. This is a test, a collection of survey results she'll present to her mother when she's ready to launch a counterargument.

"I've never thought about it." Barbara doesn't want to undermine, but really. Nail polish? How did Jenna get to be such a strict parent? There'd never been such rules when she was growing up. Jenna hadn't worn makeup; Julie had. Barbara can't remember this ever being an issue.

"But what's she like?" Barbara tries to steer the conversation back. "Your teacher. Is she nice?"

Ruby shrugs, scrunching her nose as if this is a boring question unworthy of consideration. "Can we get ice creams?"

"Not today."

"I didn't tell Mama." Ruby puffs out her chest with pride, and Barbara feels a twinge of discomfort she pushes quickly aside.

"We're going to meet my friend Stewart at the park." When Ruby seems dubious, she continues: "You remember. He let you play with his little dog."

Ruby grins. "Oh, yeah! Will she be there?"

"Yep."

For the moment, ice cream is forgotten.

In the parking lot, Barbara recognizes the beige sedan and finds an empty spot beside it. This morning, the weatherman predicted a temperature crash this weekend. The number of cars in the lot suggests they aren't alone in their desire to take advantage of the last of the nice days.

Stewart is waiting for them at the same bench. Trudy is lying at his feet, her pink tongue lolling. She jumps up and starts wagging her tail when she sees Ruby, and Stewart hands over the leash.

"Stay where we can see you!" Barbara calls to the back of Ruby's head.

Stewart leans in and kisses her cheek, and she blushes as they sit beside each other. She isn't sure how she feels about public displays, having had no reason to give the matter much thought in the last twenty years. When she'd been married to Bill, they'd enjoyed embarrassing the children with their affection for each other. Her first husband permitted nothing beyond handholding—in his case, simply a declaration of his ownership.

"I have something for you," Stewart says, holding out a brown paper bag.

Barbara takes it, grateful to have something to do with her hands. She pulls out a copy of *A Man Called Ove*.

"I thought we could start our own book club. Have you read it?"

"No." It's not true. She used to read often when she was traveling to make flights go faster. The stories blurred together and were mostly forgotten, so she won't mind the reread. She looks at the back cover, vaguely remembering that she liked it the first time.

"My son's recommendation."

"I can't wait for our first book club meeting."

He cocks an eyebrow. "I'll bring the sparkling cider!"

Barbara laughs. To be flirting at her age feels silly but also thrilling. For a moment, they sit quietly together. Ruby is sitting on the grass with her back turned, talking a blue streak to the dog. Barbara doesn't need to see the girl's lips moving; it's obvious from the flapping of her arms.

"I have a legal question for you," Barbara says.

Stewart looks at her expectantly, and she realizes she doesn't know how to start. That's how crazy everything is— she doesn't have the words. She stammers, tells things out of order, leaving sentences unfinished and circling back to the beginning. All she knows for sure is the plan can't be allowed to happen.

"I can't let her give away her baby. I have to do something."

Stewart holds his hand over his mouth, stroking his chin and scowling, deep in thought. Barbara lets herself imagine he might have a solution. "Family law was not my area of expertise," he says finally. "But from what I've seen, it can get real messy."

Barbara nods. Jenna *is* making a mess of things. "What are my rights?"

"To be honest, I don't think you have many."

"How can this be? I'm the grandmother."

"Would you be petitioning for custody?"

"Well, no. I—" Barbara falters.

"Are you prepared to call her parenting into question? Have her declared mentally unfit? In court?"

Barbara watches Ruby heading toward them, skipping, laughing. She remembers Jenna's struggle to get pregnant, Sam injecting her with hormones. She never complained—after the year of Sam's cancer treatments, she seemed to feel guilty to want anything more.

Jenna's a better mother than she ever was. Better than her mother was.

Stewart places his hands over hers, squeezes. "I'm so sorry," he says, and she nods, defeated.

Chapter Five

By December, Barbara and Stewart are on their sixth book. They take turns choosing the titles. He leans toward the classics, while she favors contemporary stuff. He's had several dinners at Jenna's house, and he met Julie over Thanksgiving. She'll meet his sons when they come home for Christmas.

He still hasn't slept in her bedroom. Whenever they have sleepovers, they go to his house because of Trudy. She usually has to go outside once during the night, and Stewart must be on alert. He's been locking her doggy door at night since she's started going blind, her big brown eyes gone foggy with cataracts.

Tonight, she whimpers at around three a.m., and he gets up quietly and shuffles down the hall to let her out. He turns on the outside floodlight so she can find her way back in the house when she's done. Barbara hears a kitchen chair scratching against tile and hopes he doesn't fall asleep at the table.

She's drifting back to sleep when she feels him slide into bed beside her. She reaches for him in the dark. "You're a good man."

"I don't mind. I'd have to get up to pee myself at some point."

He does this for his late wife, she knows. The dog is a way for him to prove his love and loyalty. "She's lucky to have you."

"She's never asked for much. She's a good dog." He doesn't know how to take a compliment. "I never had to do any of the hard stuff when she was a puppy. Potty training and basic obedience. Rita did everything. I was no help to her back then. It's my turn now."

He alludes to himself as a bad husband, back before he'd become sober. She knows he still wrestles with guilt for what he put his wife through. Apparently, he spent much of his marriage drunk, went to rehab for the first time when his boys were in junior high. His sobriety didn't stick until his wife's cancer diagnosis. She did chemo and radiation, and they had several years together when they were both healthy before the cancer came back.

But he never drank again, not even after she died, and his sons went back to their grown-up lives, and he was left alone in the house. The only responsibility he had then was Trudy, the silly dog he'd never cared for who meant so much to his wife.

It had been enough.

Barbara has such a hard time imagining him as an alcoholic, it often slips her mind. At one of their first dinners at his house, she brought a bottle of wine. She's never been a big drinker and hardly notices the absence.

Stewart's breathing shifts to a steady pace. He sleeps on the left side of the bed, closest to the door, and she's getting used to the right side. Sometimes she imagines the woman who slept here before her, and whether she'd be glad to see the space filled.

***

A year into her retirement, Barbara has let her hair grow longer. Softer.

On the day before Christmas, she goes to the salon. She wants to look her best in the holiday photos. The salon is officially closed, but Monique makes an exception for her. They have the space for themselves, which makes Barbara feel special.

Monique talked her into getting shampooed in the room at the back. It's part of the luxury of retirement, she says. More time for pampering. Barbara can't come up with a good reason to argue; she has long stretches of free time she's still figuring out what to do with. Since the kids are on Christmas break, she doesn't even have Ruby's kindergarten pickups to look forward to.

Monique squeezes a liberal dollop of conditioner into her palm. It smells like vanilla and orange blossoms. She turns off the faucet and begins to rub it through Barbara's hair. "So, do we still like the new guy?"

"He's hardly new." Barbara keeps her eyes closed for her scalp massage. "It's been four months."

"Mmhmm. So that's a yes?"

"That's a yes."

"It's nice to see you smiling. Will I get to meet him tomorrow?" Monique comes to Jenna's every year, but never stays for dinner. She has three grown children in town and must make the rounds.

"No, his sons will be home, so he's not coming. I'm going over to his place for dessert, but I'll spend the day with Will and Ruby."

"Is Will still a believer? It's not as much fun when they stop."

Barbara scowls. Will's turning twelve soon and must have kids at school giving him the lowdown on Santa. Christmas is less fun when the magic is gone. She's excited to go to Jenna's early in the morning to watch them open their stockings. She supposes there are only a few more years before the kids outgrow the rituals. "I don't know, but Ruby still believes. They leave out cookies and carrots the night before, the whole nine."

"Jenna's a good mom." Monique turns the water back on and shields Barbara's eyes from the spray.

She is. When she was still pregnant, she stitched Ruby's name on a stocking and hung it on the mantle. Barbara wonders if Liam will do this for the new baby, what the name will be.

Monique wraps Barbara's head in a towel. Her long fingernails are painted dark purple. Barbara isn't sure if they're real or not and thinks it might be rude to ask. Either way, they're pretty, and they feel great on her scalp.

The two women walk back into the main room and Barbara takes her seat at Monique's station.

"Liam will be there." Liam has always come for Christmas, since before Ruby or Marco or Sam. Barbara wonders what his plans will be next year.

"Have you seen him since the Labor Day fiasco?"

"No. And I have to make nice." Barbara remembers Julie's words that day on the lawn: *If you want to be part of their lives.* Jenna had echoed those sentiments the next time they spoke. Outwardly, Barbara has been on her best behavior, holding her tongue. She still has kidnapping fantasies, but nobody needs to know. She remembers how it felt to be disowned by her daughters, to varying degrees, and has no intention of revisiting those years. She's already living on borrowed time.

"Maybe I can help. I'll drop by before dinner." Monique opens a drawer and selects a black comb.

"Help how?"

"I could be a buffer. Or we could have a signal. You could pull on your ear or something, and I could interrupt if you're about to say something crazy."

"Oh, I'm the crazy one? What if this was your grandchild?"

"There are so many of them now, I might not notice."

Barbara sulks in silence as Monique combs through her wet hair.

"No, that was a stupid joke." Monique stops combing and meets Barbara's eyes in the mirror. "I'm sorry. It's hard, I know. But it's also an amazing thing Jenna's doing. And you'll still get to see this kid grow up. It'll just be different. Think how much more love this baby will have compared to many others."

Barbara nods and Monique twists a section of her hair into a knot and fastens it with a clip, seeming satisfied they're not arguing. She reaches for her scissors.

It's true, of course, but cold comfort. Monique is ten years younger, but much more comfortable with the speed at which the world is changing. She's been divorced since her children were small, but she manages to live in the same town as her ex-husband. They coparent and are friendly. It's all quite healthy and *mature*.

It's hard for Barbara to imagine; she hasn't had to be in the same room as her ex since she left Ohio. She spoke to him on the phone a few times when the girls were in school, and they visited him in the summers. He purchased their bus tickets, and she never felt guilty about it. She hadn't asked for child support for any of the children, and he never offered. He sent flowers when Bill died and for both girls' weddings. She isn't sure if he'd ever found out he wasn't their biological father. She certainly never thought of telling him.

Barbara thinks exes are exes for a reason, but Julie is the same, collecting former lovers as lifelong friends. It's such a foreign idea to Barbara. She isn't about to spend her golden years watching black-and-white films and longing for the good old days, but she can't help thinking not all social progress is an improvement, like expanding the basic definition of family to allow someone to give away her grandchild.

Monique runs her hands through Barbara's hair. "I didn't notice before, but it's about time to touch up your roots again. Do you have time to stay?"

She does.

***

The urn is still at the back of Barbara's closet. She sees it when she looks for the wrapping paper. Just knowing it's in her house has stirred everything up again for her; after nearly sixty years, the pain feels fresh. She thinks about James every day now, about the life he never got to have. Would he be balding or portly? Would he smoke a pipe like their father had? Would he have married a woman Barbara never thought was good enough? Lived close to let their children grow up together? Would he have grown into someone who preferred Jim or Jimmy?

She still hasn't decided what to do with the ashes, and now that the ground is frozen, she has given herself permission to set the concern aside.

She lays the gifts across her bed. For Jenna and Julie, she's chosen identical cashmere sweaters, differing in size and color. Growing up, they could never be persuaded into wearing the same outfit—not once they were old enough to express an opinion on the matter.

Somehow, she had convinced them to wear matching dresses when she married Bill, and she can still picture the five of them and a minister in the backyard. Barbara wore a tasteful ivory dress that came to her knee. Billy gave her away, then took his place next to Bill. The girls fidgeted on either side of her. They were six. Barbara's father had died that summer; her mother wasn't speaking to her. Barbara said, "I do," and thought: *This is my family now.*

Oliver hops onto the bed and heads straight for one of the open sweater boxes. When Barbara tries to shoo him away, he nips at her wrist. She imagines it would be nice to take a nap in cashmere, but she isn't such a pushover. She's become accustomed to his old-age crotchetiness, which reminds her of Bill's demeanor near the end of his life. He'd lash out in anger sometimes, but she never held it against him. Out of his control, a product of confusion. His sweetness was what made her fall in love with him. Even when they were trapped in marriages to other people, the memory of his fierce, gentle adoration made her entertain the idea she might be deserving of that kind of love.

Stewart's love might never be as fierce, but there's a familiar gentleness to it. She thinks she might be able to accept he'll never love her the way he loves Rita. She might never love him the way she loves Bill.

Lately, Barbara thinks they might be on their way to finding something different, something of their own. She's gotten him a leather bookmark, seared with his initials. He thinks Christmas is for children and said they shouldn't go *overboard* with gifts. She agonized over finding the perfect thing—intimate without being extravagant. She hates feeling like *too much* even more than *not enough*, the vulnerability of it.

She's brought educational gifts for the children—a board game about geography for Ruby and a chemistry set for Will. Billy and Sam get Red Sox gear every year, the easiest ones on her list. The sweater she chose for Jenna is roomier since she's recently popped. The first few months, she looked like she'd gotten heavier, but now you can tell she's pregnant. She's well into her second trimester, and Barbara's realizing the time to talk sense into her is slipping away. The other day, Barbara had taken a wrong turn in a department store and found herself looking at impossibly tiny baby clothes. She hadn't let herself buy anything. She wonders if this means she's resigned herself to the inevitable.

When she finishes the wrapping, she puts the packages under the tree in the living room. She doesn't usually get a tree for her own house, but this year she went to the store the day she found out Billy was coming. It's been several years since Barbara's had all her kids in one place for Christmas, something she took for granted when they were small. He can only stay two nights, but she wants him to get the full Christmas experience.

She wandered through the display of plastic trees and chose one with the lights already done, remembering how Bill spent forever untangling the string before they could hang the decorations. She doesn't have the same patience. As it is, the box sat unopened in the living room until that morning, and she'd only managed to hang a handful of ornaments before sitting down beside Oliver, worn out. Tree-trimming, she's decided, isn't a one-person activity.

Fake trees have gotten much more realistic over the last forty years, but she finds herself disappointed anyway. It doesn't smell like pine.

*****

Billy flies in at midnight and Barbara doesn't mind picking him up. She spots him breathing smoke on the curb, and he jumps in the car with a duffel bag, leaning over to kiss her cheek. She doesn't get a decent hug until he's in her kitchen. The scrawny teenager has grown into a six-foot tall, solid man, which always takes her by surprise the first few moments she's in his company again—as if one day, she might stumble upon the younger version of him at baggage claim. He came to her retirement party last year, and only stayed for a few days. She makes him a sandwich and sits across the table to watch him eat it.

"I wish you'd bring a woman home with you one of these times."

He rolls his eyes. "You're old-fashioned."

"Or a man. I don't care. I want to see you happy."

"I am happy."

Now, Barbara rolls her eyes. "But you should be settled down." She thinks about his hip apartment with its exposed brick, leather couches, one bedroom. She'd only visited him there once, years ago. With all her business trips, she'd had many layovers in the Chicago airport, but he could never meet her for lunch. After a while, she stopped asking.

When she visited, he took a day off and they went to the museum. They'd had a lovely day, but he hadn't introduced her to anyone from his life.

"Who do you have to make you sandwiches in Chicago?" she asks.

"I don't have time for sandwiches in Chicago."

"You don't have time for sandwiches?" Without meaning to, Barbara finds herself shifting her gaze to his ample midsection.

He laughs at her apparent incredulity, never one to take offense. Barbara remembers walking on eggshells when the girls were teenagers, such a contrast to Billy's easy nature. "I'm a busy guy. Not everyone needs to settle down."

"But don't you want to settle down? You can't put it off a whole lot longer."

"I'm not putting it off. It's not on the list. I love my job and my friends and my alone time. The last thing this world needs is more babies."

"Maybe you should tell your sister. She's gotten tired of having her own babies, now she's having them for other people."

"It's probably not my place to tell her." He's quiet for a moment, chewing. Then he glances over at her, sharply. "Or yours."

Barbara frowns.

"Hey, you got to choose how you wanted to use your genetic material. We get to decide about ours—whether we keep it, give it away, or flush it down a toilet."

Barbara gasps and makes a face. "Don't be gross."

Billy shrugs and pops the last bite of sandwich into his mouth.

***

It's too late to fall asleep, knowing she'll need be awake in a few hours, but Barbara lies in her bed and closes her eyes. Billy wants to sleep in. He'll get a ride over with Julie, but Jenna has promised to text as soon as the kids are up so Barbara can come over.

Barbara had always had to go to church growing up, and later, in Ohio. The first Christmas after she moved back to New England, she'd gone to her parent's house in Boothbay, and they'd been forced to pause in their merriment to dress up for mass, first dresses and tights—and a plaid clip-on tie for Billy—then hats and scarves and mittens to face the cold winter morning. It was a chore.

Finally, on her first Christmas married to Bill, she was able to spend the holiday the way *she* wanted. They opened stockings, and then Bill fried eggs and bacon and when they were full, they sat around the Christmas tree and opened all their gifts. She wore pajamas all day and watched out the bay window in the living room while the children played in the snow.

The memory of each Christmas blurs together, as though they were always the same and always would be.

But then Billy moved to Chicago, and Bill died, and Julie ran away, and Jenna started a family of her own. Barbara was lucky to be invited over for a glimpse.

Chapter Six

By seven a.m., Jenna's living room is strewn with discarded wrapping paper. Will has disappeared to the basement to play a new video game, and Ruby has fallen asleep sitting up on the couch holding two new dolls in her lap.

Barbara tiptoes around the kitchen, loading the dishwasher quietly. Sam tries to take over, but she shoos him away. "Where's Jenna?"

"She went upstairs to lie down for a while." He leans against the counter, reaching for a piece of bacon left to cool on a paper towel. "Every year, we swear we won't go nuts, but we always do."

"What do you mean?" She closes the dishwasher lightly and turns toward him.

He waves around his hand. "The excess. We buy everything on their list. It's kind of gross." He shrugs. "I wasn't raised like this. Some years, we didn't get gifts."

"Oh, wow. That must have been hard."

Sam chuckles. "I don't mean we were poor," he says. "My mom was always switching religions, so sometimes we didn't celebrate."

Barbara nods. His mother is a character; she'll be over later. Sam holds out a slice of bacon and she takes it. Earlier, he made pancakes for everyone.

"It'll be our own fault when they turn out spoiled."

"Aww." Barbara shakes her head. "It's one day a year," she protests. "They're only little for such a short time."

It's funny; this feels like an argument she'd had with Bill when her children were small, only she was always on the other side of it. He stayed up late on Christmas Eve, putting together bicycles and dollhouses. She thought they were setting them up for disappointment in their adult lives. He wanted them to have perfect childhoods with memories that would sustain them through whatever hardships the future held. All of them: Billy as much as the girls.

Barbara knows it's the same for Sam: Ruby is his every bit as much as Will.

"It sure does go fast," Sam says, never one to disagree directly with his mother-in-law. Perhaps this is part of why Barbara likes him so much. He feels as close to her as any of her children, but without any of the baggage or conflict she has with them.

"This baby could be a new beginning for you and Jenna."

He looks down and shakes his head. His soft laughter is a product of discomfort, a struggle to maintain politeness. "This baby will be a beginning for Liam and Marco. Jenna and I are excited for them."

"Are you really going to be able to watch Jenna give up her child?" Barbara asks.

He flinches, and Barbara's glad she caught him off guard. She imagines he's more likely to be honest.

"I really am," he says to her disappointment. "Jenna and I are done with diapers and three a.m. feedings. We have the family we want."

Barbara nods, another potential ally biting the dust.

Sam decides to run the dishwasher to have clean dishes for dinner. He encourages her to nap in Ruby's room before everyone starts to arrive.

Barbara slides into the twin bed, trying to leave space beside her in case Ruby wakes in the living room and decides to come upstairs. She's tired but doesn't think she can fall asleep. She feels unsettled and agitated. Her children seem immune to her judgements of their lives. Billy feels no need to marry; Jenna will give away her child; Julie had announced her divorce as an afterthought one afternoon three years ago, over the phone.

Barbara's father believed divorce was only for extreme circumstances, an option for battered women, and then, only if the church counseling didn't work or the woman feared for her life. Barbara understood she could only leave her husband if he beat her. It was not enough that he made her feel small and scared and empty, that he made her feel like nothing, like love was something other people deserved.

Had Barbara cared too much about what her parents thought of her? She had run away from them once and didn't want to admit her marriage had been a mistake, to give them the satisfaction of being right. Fear of hearing *I told you so* had trapped her in Ohio for years. Although, in the end, she had left.

Barbara's father had raged over her divorce, but eventually, he seemed to ignore it. For the year after she moved back from Ohio, her parents acted like her husband was simply off at work when she visited with the children. Perhaps they expected her to return to him. When she announced her plans to remarry, her father's rage returned.

In the eyes of God, he explained, she was already married and would be for life. God didn't care about the paperwork or whether she chose to live in a different state. There was only one husband she would ever have: the father of her children.

When her father revealed his belief that her children had been fathered by the same man, Barbara realized her mother had never told him about the afternoon seven years before, when she'd been discovered with Bill in the neighbor's brass bed. Her mother must have decided he couldn't handle it.

She'd been right. If only Barbara hadn't felt the need to correct him, much would be different.

***

The day does not go to plan. Julie's alarm doesn't go off and she doesn't arrive with Billy until two. Dinner's at four. Monique helps Barbara set the tables—there are two. Jenna has decided both her siblings will dine at the "kids' table" with Ruby and Will. The main table is set for six.

Monique folds the cloth napkins into flower shapes as Barbara follows behind with silverware. Then they sit on either side of Ruby to paint her fingernails red and green. The hardest part is reminding her to keep still while the polish dries.

The timing is off again when Monique is heading out as Liam arrives with Marco and an older woman. Everyone exchanges kisses and handshakes at the door, whichever is appropriate. The introductions and goodbyes overlap.

"Liam's mother, Nancy," Barbara hears Jenna tell Monique. The woman has long, gray-blond hair and wears a fussy purple scarf she takes several long moments unwinding. Sam takes an armful of winter coats to a back bedroom as Monique is putting on a pair of black leather gloves.

Nancy reaches for Jenna, both hands caressing her stomach with a hunger that makes Barbara woozy.

"Nan's here!" Jenna calls, and the children come running.

"Ruby, you're so big!" the woman sing-songs, and Barbara follows Monique outside. She's forgotten her own coat, and the cold doesn't hit her until she's standing beside Monique's car at the side of the road.

"Take a breath," Monique says before Barbara realizes she's been holding it.

"Did you see the way she grabbed Jenna's belly?"

Monique nods slowly, her hand on the car door handle. "She's excited."

"Proprietary." Barbara stomps her feet to get her circulation going.

"She's going to be a grandmother. Remember how that feels."

Jenna said she hated the way people felt entitled to touch her when she was pregnant, even strangers. Barbara had learned to ask first.

"The kids call her Nan?"

"Her name is Nancy."

Barbara rolls her eyes. They call Sam's mom Grammy. Barbara has always thought Nana sounds, not younger, exactly, but sort of ageless.

"It's too cold for this." Monique pulls the car door open. Barbara wishes she could ask her to stay. She can't; Monique has her own dinner to get to. She's already running late. "Go inside." She shuts the door, starts the engine, and lowers the window. "And be nice."

Barbara frowns at her as she drives away. Monique offers more tough love than she wishes, never one to coddle or humor her. Sometimes, this feels disloyal. *Be on my side*, she wants to say. It shouldn't matter whether she's right.

If it wasn't so cold, she might not go inside. But she takes the front steps slowly, teeth chattering.

The men have moved to the basement with Will; the women are in the living room. Barbara hovers in the doorway. The furniture has been rearranged. This morning, all the seating was facing the tree; now, the seats face each other, encouraging conversation. Ruby sits on Nancy's lap, the woman's hands clasped tightly around the girl's waist.

Barbara sits down across from them on the couch next to Julie, who's telling a story about her most recent renovation project. Barbara always struggles to imagine Julie climbing a ladder to wield a hammer on a rooftop. She spent her teen years at the mall, collecting fashion magazines, doing her hair. Now, she wears practical shoes and keeps her nails short. She spent Christmas Eve installing bathroom tiles.

Jenna stands to go check on the turkey, one hand braced behind her, back arched, leading with her belly button. Nancy's gaze follows. "I still remember those days like they were yesterday," she says. "I loved being pregnant." She turns to Barbara. "Didn't you?"

"Oh, god, no," Barbara blurts out and Julie laughs. "I was fat, sick, and exhausted, and my ankles hurt. It was awful."

"I've never understood why women put themselves through it," Julie says. "I mean, kids are a dime a dozen. If you really want one, there are a zillion in foster care. No offense, Ruby."

Ruby sticks out her tongue, and Julie reaches out to pinch her cheek. Barbara isn't sure how much Ruby understands, aside from the fact her aunt is teasing her.

"I'm gonna go find one of those brownies I saw earlier," Julie says.

"We're going to eat dinner soon," Barbara protests reflexively.

Julie sighs as she stands. "The best thing about being a grown up is your mother can't tell you not to ruin your appetite." She points at Ruby. "Thirteen more years for you. Hang in there."

"You're a bad influence," Barbara tells her, but she shrugs as she heads to the kitchen.

Ruby sends Barbara a pleading look.

"Ask your mother," she replies.

Nancy releases her grip and Ruby hops down, running out of the room before anyone can change their mind.

There's a beat of awkward silence as the two women are left alone in the room. Barbara forces a smile. "One of the best grandmother tricks: never having to be the bad guy."

Nancy smiles back. "You must get to see them often since you live in town."

"More, since I retired," Barbara says. "How often do you get to visit Liam?"

"Not as much as I'd like."

"How far away are you?"

"I'm over in Connecticut, but I teach at a private school, and most of our vacations are at different times." As Nancy talks, she fiddles with the buttons on her blue cardigan. She clears her throat and lowers her voice. "The truth is, we've had a few difficult years, recently."

"Oh?"

"I didn't meet Ruby until she was three." She shakes her head. "I didn't approve or understand, I guess. It was hard."

"It *is* hard," Barbara says. Until this moment, she'd been looking at this woman as an adversary, a competitor. Suddenly, she is the only person who understands.

"Ruby would have been my first grandchild." Barbara takes a moment to imagine this, whether it would have made her crazier if Jenna had planned to give Will away. "She looks much like Liam did at that age." Nancy reaches to pinch the bridge of her nose, blinking back tears. "This will be the first grandchild I can claim."

Not one to touch strangers, Barbara struggles with the urge to reach out. She folds her arms tightly across her chest, and the urge passes. What she feels toward Nancy is more complicated than sympathy, more layered. They're in the same boat, but there aren't enough life vests to worry about anyone else. Perhaps there aren't any life vests at all.

She's reminded of the days and weeks and months after Bill died. She knew the children were in pain, but her own grief was all-consuming and blotted them out. In truth, she resented having to consider their pain at all. This has made her resist the idea of emotional support groups. It's appealing to know someone understands what you're going through, but ultimately, you must understand what they're going through, too, and acknowledge that their experience matters as much as yours. These groups require you to give up the view of yourself as the most important. Barbara doesn't want to do this.

When Barbara's in pain, she doesn't care about anyone else's pain. Nancy wants to claim this grandchild, which means Barbara cannot.

"It seems like our children want to break everything apart and come up with their own definitions for things that have been the same for millions of years," Barbara says.

Nancy nods. "It's scary," she says. "But it's also kind of brave, I think." This time, her smile is crooked.

Barbara isn't sure these things can be easily redefined. Bravery or hubris? And what happens if they're wrong? The children will suffer the most. And the grandmothers.

Jenna comes to the door, wisps of hair loose from her ponytail clinging to her damp forehead. "The turkey is done. Who's hungry?"

**

By the time Barbara gets to Stewart's house, it's clear everyone's holiday cheer is wearing thin. His four grandchildren are in their teens: they're zoning out to a movie in the dimly lit living room. They briefly lift their heads from the screen as Barbara is introduced from the doorway.

Stewart hangs her coat in the front hallway and kisses her on the mouth. He leads her into the dining room where his sons and their wives are slumped around the dining room table with cups of coffee. They brighten at her arrival, seeming desperate for a new source of conversation.

They start with introductions. His sons are Paul and Martin. The wives are Sally and Ellen.

"It's nice to finally put faces to the names. Stewart talks about you all the time."

"More pie!" Sally exclaims over the dish in Barbara's hands.

"Oh no, should I have brought something else?"

"No way! There's no such thing as too much pie. What kind you got?"

There's no way to pretend it's anything other than what it is: a store-bought pumpkin pie. She tells them about the one she made from scratch yesterday, how someone had taken it from the pantry to serve. They'd meant well. She should have left it in the car. Lucky to have found anything open on Christmas day.

Stewart pulls gently on her arm. "Let's go slice it up in the kitchen."

Along the counter, there are three other pies: apple, pecan, and blueberry. Stewart grabs a fistful of silverware and slams the drawer shut.

"You lie about things that don't matter," he says.

Barbara looks at him, surprised. She doesn't know how to respond, whether a denial would only make things worse.

He passes her a triangular knife, the kind made specifically for cutting pies, something she has never owned. "I'll go ask the kids which kind they want." He leaves the room without clarifying which group he considers *kids*. Maybe both.

She looks down at her hands, wondering if this knife had been a wedding gift or something his wife purchased. Perhaps she'd done a lot of baking. Barbara cuts the pumpkin pie into eight slices.

When Stewart returns, he says, "Three blueberry; one apple," and he takes the knife away from her and asks her to find the vanilla ice cream in the freezer. She reaches in the drawer for a big spoon, and he shakes his head, opens a different drawer and retrieves an ice cream scoop.

"Should we exchange gifts before we eat?" Barbara asks, hoping to do this in private.

"Sure. I'll bring yours when I come back." He leaves with an armful of plates, and Barbara finds the small rectangular box in her purse.

He comes back with orders from the dining room and an envelope. "The boys are asking for two slices each, and the ladies only want *a sliver*."

Barbara is amused that he imagines his sons, pushing fifty, are boys and their wives are ladies. She supposes she's the same; her *girls* are turning forty in April. She hands him the box and watches as he opens it. He tears the paper neatly and sets it aside. He holds the bookmark, running his thumb over the depression his initials make in the leather.

"It's great," he says. "Thank you."

"You're quite welcome."

"I guess we had the same idea," he says as she opens her gift card to the local book shop. Barbara has only ever purchased gift certificates for employees she doesn't know personally.

Stewart leans in for a quick peck and turns back to the pies as Barbara turns away and slips her gift in her purse. She swallows a lump in her throat, angry she let herself think this was something more than what it is. Imagining they were building something solid, possibly permanent when, clearly, he's filling time with her. He has no intention of getting to know her, of thinking about what sort of small bauble would make her smile. If she'd realized this, she never would have let him get to know her family; she wouldn't have come to meet his sons tonight.

Stewart asks what kind of pie she wants, though anyone who paid any attention at all would already know.

Barbara sighs and takes three of the plates from the counter, plastering a smile on her face and steeling herself to get through the rest of the evening.

Chapter Seven

In the morning, Billy takes one look at his mother and offers to get an Uber to the airport.

"Don't be silly," Barbara says, pitching her voice higher, as though she might project a youthful energy to negate the bags under her eyes. She left Stewart's by nine o'clock, citing her lack of sleep the night before, but last night had been no better. "I'm not letting some taxi driver have your last minutes in New Hampshire." She opens her arms to hug him, stands on her tiptoes. "I wish you could stay longer."

"You should visit," he says.

"Maybe when it's warmer." When Barbara thinks of Chicago in the winter, she thinks of stories she's heard about the wind, the uninhabitable cold. As an adult, she traveled endlessly for her job, always scheduling trips around the weather: D.C. and Chicago in the summer, L.A. and Phoenix in the winter. The younger version of herself would never have imagined how frequent a traveler she would become. Ohio had seemed exotic to a girl of seventeen who'd never been farther than Boston, in fact had only been to two other states. Not even Vermont. And once she'd moved there, it seemed far away. Now people travel between coasts with such ease it's no longer the end of the world when your child takes a job halfway across the country.

Billy zips his jacket all the way up and tucks his chin inside as he heads out the front door. Barbara steps where he has stepped, hoping the dark pavement in the driveway isn't secretly icy. It snowed earlier in the month, but, for now, the lawn is bare. Barbara wishes for snow, something positive to balance out the negative of the cold. By March, she will see it all as negative, desperately wishing the dirty snow piles along the roadside would melt.

They pass three Dunkin' Donuts before finding one open twenty-four hours. Jenna had worked there in the summers through college, and it still stirs a sense of brand loyalty for Barbara as though it's a family business. Bill's favorite had been the Boston Kreme, one of the few foods he still got excited for near the end.

Barbara orders two coffees and two glazed donuts. She thanks the girl at the window and hands the bag to Billy, arranges the drinks in the cup holder. He adds sugar to his as she drives, imagining hers will be too hot to drink until well past the time she drops him off.

"I had a good time talking with Jenna and Julie last night after everyone left or went to bed." Billy holds his cup, blowing against the steam.

"That's nice." Barbara is on alert immediately. This is the sort of innocuous small talk her son eschews, especially this early in the morning.

"They said we had an uncle?"

Barbara turns on her blinker. There's a blue truck coming down the main road. She waits for it to pass. "I'm not sure I'd call him that. He died before you were born."

"Well, you had a brother, then."

"James."

"And he died quite young?"

"He was three." Barbara keeps her voice flat.

"Have you decided what you want to do with the ashes?"

Barbara shakes her head. She notices he doesn't ask the kind of questions paramount to his sisters: the *how* and *why* questions.

"If you want to have a service for him, I could talk to the priest from Grammy's church. Maybe this summer I could fly home, and we could have some kind of memorial as a family."

The idea of doing something public has never occurred to her. The road blurs as she follows the blue airplane signs, turning right.

"Would you like that?" Billy asks.

Barbara clears her throat. "I don't know how your grandmother would feel."

"Who cares how she'd feel? She's dead." The anger in his voice seems to surprise him too. He pauses before continuing more quietly. "You don't have to keep her secrets anymore."

Is this what she's been doing? After all these years, this feels like her secret, her shame. She told the girls he had drowned, but nothing more, nothing about her complicity. There is no longer a single person alive who knows the truth of what happened, no one besides herself. The truth exists in her mind alone, and if she never says it aloud, it almost doesn't exist at all.

Barbara pulls the car tight against the curb. The sky is brightening to a light shade of gray. She turns to her son.

"What a sweet idea. I'll think about it." It isn't a lie, exactly. She means the first part.

***

The coffee is cool enough to drink by the time Barbara gets to Jenna's house. All these years, they've lived in the same town, but Barbara knows it had nothing to do with Jenna wanting to stay close to her mother and everything to do with Sam. The two had met the fall before Bill died, when Jenna had come home to help. Bill liked Sam immediately, seeming to know before anyone else Sam would be sticking around long after Bill was gone.

Bill died in November, and the grief was still fresh by Thanksgiving. That year, Jenna and Julie insisted on making a turkey with all the fixings, including the green bean casserole only Bill had liked. Underlining his absence in every moment was awful. Barbara had decided to go on a cruise for Christmas, to pretend the holiday didn't exist—a stupid plan, as the ship was full of celebrating families. There was a differently decorated tree around every corner, Santa in red shorts on every deck.

Maybe she should have felt more guilty about leaving the girls at Christmas, but honestly, she didn't. Losing a father is a generic loss, something most people live through. And the twins had each other. What Barbara was going through was an entirely different quality of grief. She had lost the only person in her whole life who ever actually loved her. He knew everything about her, and he loved her anyway. He was crazy about her. No one would ever love her like that again—this wasn't something her daughters could understand.

They also couldn't understand that for her, Bill's loss had been coming in waves for two years by then, the first one knocking her down after his first heart surgery, when his brain had gone without oxygen for too long. He came home with a sweet form of dementia which made Barbara imagine what he'd been like as a boy. He couldn't drive or do simple math or remember things he'd been told the day before. He was no longer her peer, never mind her partner. They hadn't made love since his diagnosis.

So, there'd been other men, mostly married ones who didn't ask much of her. All she wanted from them was the ability to close her eyes, feel the weight of a man on her body, and pretend she wasn't alone. She'd taken one with her on the cruise, as a distraction. He'd dumped her at the airport before the flight back, and she was horrified he'd beat her to it.

She drank on the plane and took a cab home. She'd been relieved to come back to an empty house, and it didn't dawn on her to wonder why. She had found a bottle of wine and was drinking in the dark when Jenna's car pulled into the drive. Her memory of their conversation has always been hazy, but that was the night all her lies caught up to her. In fact, they'd known for months; Bill's deathbed confession was followed by DNA tests and didn't leave much wiggle room.

By winter, Jenna was back in school and barely speaking to Barbara, but she came back to town to see Sam, who processed loans at the bank where he still works. He's a manager now. If he hadn't been here, drawing her back, Jenna might have taken off the way Julie did. As it was, Jenna and Barbara met for dinner sporadically at first, then more often, having strained conversations about Jenna's graduate school classes and the weather.

After a day and a half, Barbara noticed Bill's dog was missing—long enough to prove she wasn't responsible enough to care for him and too long to feign indignance over the loss. She'd learn later Sam had taken him in.

When she sees the upstairs light flicker on, Barbara turns off the car engine. After a few minutes, the light goes out again, and the kitchen light comes on. Barbara brings her coffee with her to the front door.

Jenna pulls the door open before Barbara can knock; she must have heard the car door slam. "What's wrong?" she asks, pulling her robe closed at her throat.

"Nothing. I dropped your brother at the airport."

"Oh." She sighs, relieved. "I knew he was flying out early, but this is godawful." Barbara comes inside and Jenna pushes the door closed with both hands.

Barbara shrugs. "I feel like I just picked him up." She follows Jenna into the kitchen.

"This is what happens when you're a fancy doctor, in demand."

"Is that what it is?" Barbara sits at the kitchen table without taking off her coat.

Jenna scowls. "Of course. What else?"

"Only two days for Christmas?"

"If anyone should understand work being a priority, it's you."

"Why does he need to live far away? There are doctors in New Hampshire."

Jenna leans against the counter with her arms folded across her chest, her belly poking out from her robe.

Beside her, the coffee machine begins to percolate. "Aw, Mom."

"What?"

"Nothing." Jenna gets the mugs down from the cabinet by the sink. Barbara doesn't press, knowing it's probably something she wouldn't want to hear.

Barbara sulks. Sam comes downstairs in a suit and tie.

"Speaking of workaholics," Jenna says.

"Who, me?" Sam kisses the top of her head and starts making a bagel. "No way. I'd make a super trophy husband."

"Oh, yeah?"

"Totally. I'd sleep in and watch sports all day in my boxers. Then you could take me out for dinner and show me off to all your friends." Sam pushes out his stomach and wiggles his hips.

Jenna laughs. "Ah. I'll keep that in mind."

Sam squeezes Barbara's shoulder. "I thought I heard people talking down here."

"Mom took Billy to the airport." Jenna carries her mug to the table and sits down. "Hey, if you're home all day, you'll clean the house and stuff?"

Sam shakes his head, emphatically. "That's some workaholic shit right there. Nice try. Can't cut into my bonbon eating time."

"Twenty-five cents for the jar, Dad," Will says from the doorway.

"No fair! I didn't know you were up!"

"What *are* you doing up this early?" Barbara asks.

Will shrugs and takes the seat next to her. He's wearing the same X-Men t-shirt and pajama bottoms he wore all day yesterday.

"Probably has something to do with how early you went to bed," Jenna says.

He shrugs again. "Can I have Cream of Wheat?" he asks, and Jenna gets up to make it.

Barbara raises an eyebrow. "His legs broke?"

"It's his vacation," Jenna says.

"When's your vacation?"

"Moms don't get vacation," she says, keeping her voice light. "But it's okay. I knew when I signed up."

The toaster releases Sam's bagel and he smears it with cream cheese, presses the halves together, and holds it in his mouth as he puts on his jacket, sticks his briefcase under his arm, and carries his coffee to the door, calling out muffled goodbyes.

Jenna presses buttons on the microwave and sits down across from Barbara. "How was last night?"

"Oh, fine," Barbara tells herself she can't get into the specifics in front of Will.

"What did he get you?"

Without missing a beat, Barbara talks about the beautiful silk scarf she'd admire once while she and Stewart were out Christmas shopping for other people, and how he went back later to get it.

"Ooh, that's worth points. Shows he pays attention."

Barbara agrees.

The microwave beeps, and Jenna stands to retrieve Will's breakfast. She places the bowl on the table in front of Will along with a spoon and the maple syrup.

"Are you guys going to Julie's for New Year's Eve?" Julie has had a party every year for a while now, but Barbara has never gone because her mother would be there. This is the first year she'll be able to attend, and she'd been looking forward to bringing Stewart along.

"I will," Barbara says. "But I don't think Stewart can make it."

***

She must do it in person. If she were younger, she could send an email or text. Or, better yet, she could *ghost* him. She'd read an article about this—about how different millennial dating is; they can stop returning messages and pretend an entire relationship never existed.

But this is not how adults behave. Instead, she manages to avoid him until Friday, after his sons leave. Then she shows up on his doorstep, claiming she was in the neighborhood. When he leans in to kiss her, she turns her head, and he kisses her cheek.

And he knows.

"Can we talk?" Barbara says.

He leads her into the living room, and they sit on the couch with the proper amount of breakup distance between them. He hasn't asked to take her coat. He's wearing khakis and a wool cardigan. She holds her purse in her lap. The room is lit dimly by a table lamp in the corner.

"I thought things were going well," he says preemptively, and she reaches out to pat his hand, feeling pity for him.

And another feeling: better him than her.

"It's been lovely," she says, smiling sadly as his face sags. It's ego, she reminds herself. He hasn't seen this coming. Later, he'll wish he had beaten her to it.

"Is it something I did?"

She shakes her head, seeing no need to go into details and expose her sensitivity. The plan is to make a clean break, get in and out as quickly as possible.

"This seems sudden."

"I'm sorry," Barbara says. "It's no one's fault. I think we want different things."

"Do we?" Stewart's eyes roam the room wildly. "What do you want?" He takes her hand with both of his, holding tightly.

Barbara is surprised by the emotion in his voice and the intensity of his eye contact. She pulls her hand away.

Stewart turns his body from her and speaks toward the carpet. "You seem to have made up your mind. Is there anything I can say?"

He's bent forward, shoulders slouched, defeated. She can see his bald spot. She resists an urge to reach for him, swallows the lump in her throat. "No. This is what I want." Her voice sounds less certain than she'd planned.

He sighs, and silence swells between them. "Okay, then," he says finally, and he gets to his feet.

Barbara stands and follows him to the door. They wish each other well and hug goodbye awkwardly.

She drives away in tears. She pulls the car over when she's racked with sobs. Barbara is not a crier; it has been years since she cried about anything at all. She tries to convince herself that the adrenaline about the dreaded confrontation is to blame. She wipes her face with the edge of her sweater and tries to get her breathing under control. The conversation went as planned: a quick in and out. Probably less than ten minutes. What she wanted. And, anyway, it's done.

Barbara turns on her left blinker and slips back into traffic, heading home, back to the way things were.

Chapter Eight

Because it's been so long since she has felt this way, Barbara can't identify the feeling at first. She thinks she might be coming down with something and worries about missing Julie's party. She spends the weekend in bed, drinking grape juice and popping vitamin C. Oliver seems to approve of the change of pace. He curls up on her chest in the afternoon, purring as she strokes his back. He's getting skinnier, she thinks. The bones of his spine seem more noticeable as he vibrates under her touch. He pushes his face into hers as she rubs the thin velvet of his ears, and his purring slows as he falls asleep, causing Barbara to be unable to move and disturb him.

In her half sleep, she replays the summer with Bill in Boothbay, and her return to Ohio that August. Billy had broken his arm in a fall from a tree, caused by a lack of parenting her husband seemed to see as an indictment of her, not of himself. He insisted they make love the night she returned; she'd shirked her wifely duties long enough. The next morning, she first suspected she was pregnant and knew the timing didn't add up. She spent the next few weeks in terror her husband would find out and she'd be abandoned, or he wouldn't find out and she'd be forced to stay.

In those weeks, she never heard from Bill. She imagined he'd gone back to his wife and put their tryst behind him. Meanwhile, her husband was becoming more and more religious, reading aloud passages from the Bible after dinner, instead of watching television. When she considered her options, she had to admit he was a decent provider, while she had barely finished high school and never had a job besides babysitting. She couldn't leave him. She had nowhere to go.

In September, she told him she was pregnant, and they prayed together on their knees, thanked God for the blessing. In the middle of the night, after he'd fallen asleep, Barbara crept from bed to stare at herself in the bathroom mirror, whispering accusations. She was a liar and a whore, and she had been an idiot to think she had found someone to love her. She was twenty-six and already felt like she had made all the choices she'd be allotted in this life, and, though she'd made a mess of it, what's done was done.

She sobbed hysterically at her reflection, pulling at her long hair, the strands Bill had wound around his fingers as they lay together in the brass bed. Heartbroken, but sure she deserved all the pain and worse, Barbara cut off her hair, forcing herself to stare at her ugly, puffy, tear-streaked face.

She wakes up in the afternoon, feeling the familiar pang deep in her chest. She's surprised by it, not having thought she was capable of such a thing. Forty years on, and she's still making a mess of it. She's alone in bed. Even Oliver has found somewhere else to be.

On the bedside table, her cell phone vibrates and flashes in the dim bedroom. She reaches for it, a text from Jenna, inviting her to dinner. She considers begging off, pulling the pillow over her head and hiding out for one more day.

Instead, she sends back a thumbs-up emoji and forces herself out of bed with a groan with only a partial relationship to her joints.

***

The weather forecast is the major topic of conversation at dinner. Will can't decide whether to be happy to get snow on his vacation or if it's a waste of what would otherwise be a snow day. Jenna worries about making the drive to Boothbay in the snow. Sam assures her it's fine; he got snow tires for the minivan.

"Can I stay up for the toast this year?" Will looks back and forth between his parents as they look at each other. "I'm almost twelve!" he adds, as if the number is substantial, a meaningful detail that slipped their minds.

Something imperceptible passes within the eye contact between Jenna and Sam. "You can try." Jenna gives a single shoulder shrug, and Will celebrates his win by making a fist and pumping his elbow back toward his waist.

"Can I be excused?"

Sam looks over his son's plate, which is mostly empty. "Fine."

Ruby looks up wide-eyed from her own plate. She's been rearranging her peas, hiding them under mashed potatoes. "What about me?"

"Three more bites," Sam says, and Ruby sighs dramatically.

Will carries his plate to the sink, and Sam begins clearing the table.

"Do you want to ride up with us?" Jenna asks.

"It's okay." Barbara doesn't have snow tires, but she's lived in the northeast for forty years, and snowstorms don't scare her.

Will thunders up the stairs, and Ruby whimpers. "You're fine," Jenna says. Ruby hates being left alone at the table. Barbara understands. She remembers staring at a plate of lima beans for hours before her father finally took pity on her and threw them away so she could go to bed, knowing he'd anger her mother. He'd been her hero that night and many others, when he'd step between them and say quietly: "Enough." A shame he could only protect her in the evenings.

Barbara never forced her children to clean their plates. "It's okay, Ruby. I won't leave until you're done."

Ruby arranges a small forkful of mashed potato and swallows. "That's one," she says.

"Fine," Jenna agrees. She reaches for the phone buzzing in her back pocket. "Oh, Liam and Marco are going to the party too," she says, reading the screen.

Ruby looks up from her plate. "Nan too?"

"No, Nan went back to her house last week."

"How often does she see Ruby?" Barbara asks, trying to sound casual.

"She lives in Connecticut," Jenna says, missing the point or pretending to.

"That's two!" Ruby shouts, and Jenna shushes her.

Sam wanders back from the sink and starts rubbing Jenna's shoulders. "There's a pan soaking. I'll get it later."

"You've got a deal."

He leaves the room as Will returns. "When is it supposed to start snowing?"

"Not for hours." Jenna stands. "You'll be asleep." She pulls the bag of trash from the basket. She finds a pair of flip-flops by the door and begins to step into them in her stocking feet.

"Jenna, don't be ridiculous!" Barbara scolds. "It's too cold out for flip-flops. Let Will take the trash out. He has real shoes on."

Will turns to his mother, looking panicked. Jenna touches his shoulder and lets him off the hook with a quick shake of the head.

"Chores are good for children," Barbara says. "Teaches work ethic. Responsibility. He should learn some self-sufficiency. When you were his age, you did your own laundry."

"Oh, yes, we were self-sufficient."

Barbara catches Jenna's tone and presses her lips together. "Fine. Let me do it then."

"Nono, you promised to stay with me," Ruby pipes up.

"Finish up. It's only one more bite," she says, but there's no point. Jenna is already in the living room, opening the slider to the backyard. She's coming back inside before Barbara can yell at her to put on a coat at least.

"And that's three!" Barbara announces, reaching across the table for Ruby's plate. She ignores her granddaughter's little puzzled face and carries the plate to the sink, rinsing the evidence down the disposal.

***

The weathermen are wrong. The first thing Barbara does when she wakes is pull aside the heavy bedroom curtains and look out the window. She feels Will's disappointment.

She takes a long bath, something she's gotten into the habit of since her retirement. She doesn't bring a book or turn on the radio. She's trying to get used to the stillness, the quiet.

When Bill retired, he'd stayed busy with various renovation projects. He pulled out the upstairs carpet and installed Pergo. He redid the whole kitchen, laying floor tiles on his hands and knees. He'd done their bathroom last, putting in a beautiful deep tub they never used—the final project before he became ill.

The winter after Bill died, Barbara started traveling more. She couldn't bear the silence of the empty house. She didn't see Julie again for three years, receiving threadbare updates on her life from Jenna. She was working for Habitat for Humanity in Louisiana, then Texas. By the summer of Jenna's wedding, Julie was living with her grandmother in Maine. They'd spoken awkwardly at the reception, while Julie's lavender bridesmaid dress was tied up at her hip to make it easier to dance. Their conversations might always be somewhat awkward.

It was better with Jenna. Those first years, Barbara had been merely tolerated, but something significant had changed around the time Will was born. Perhaps becoming a mother herself made Jenna more understanding of imperfection.

As the water starts to cool, Barbara uses her toes to turn on the hot water. Her fingertips are like prunes. There are a limited number of New Year's Eve parties left to change the story her daughters will tell of their mother, especially Julie. These thoughts about her mortality have become more frequent since her own mother died, setting their story in stone.

***

Arriving last, as intended, Barbara parks on the street and takes a headcount by looking at the other cars. Jenna's minivan, Liam's Prius, Rick's nice SUV. Hooley's beat-up truck, the name of his garage painted across the side. He's been the owner for over a decade, but Barbara still thinks of him as the grease monkey who broke her daughter's heart. There's a white light in each of the windows of her mother's house, a wreath of poinsettias on the door. Growing up, her father had always strung colored lights along the outline of the roof and windows. It looked like a gingerbread house.

It's Jenna who comes to the door. They're playing Nat King Cole, and Julie is laughing with the children. The mood is different from the last time Barbara was here. Sam offers to make her a cocktail, and she follows him into the kitchen where he's set up a makeshift bar.

"Can you do a martini?"

"Yep. I have the fun glasses, too," he says. "And olives, but no onions. Is that okay?"

Barbara nods. It seems silly to admit she's never had a martini. Whenever she's been to a bar, she orders a glass of wine.

"Is that the scarf Stewart bought you?" Jenna asks.

Barbara touches the silk at her throat: a soft green with deep purple butterflies. "Oh, yes." Eventually, she will tell her about the breakup, Jenna will spread the word to the others, and Barbara won't need to speak of it again.

She follows Jenna into the living room. Will and Ruby are sitting on the floor, too close to the television set, watching celebrities in Times Square. Barbara sits on a rectangular ottoman behind them and strokes Ruby's hair. Will is already too old for prolonged affection, but Ruby leans into it.

The volume of the television is kept low so the adults can talk. Barbara doesn't recognize any of the bundled stars and hasn't since before Dick Clark died. After his stroke, she found it too painful to watch him stutter through the brief segments he still hosted. He reminded her of Bill at the end, his wide-eyed nervousness as he struggled to prove himself capable of a once-familiar task.

They begin a game of Pictionary; Barbara passes and escapes to the kitchen to get another drink. This time, she pours herself a glass of wine. She leans against the refrigerator and listens to the laughter from the other room as she realizes she hasn't seen Hooley yet.

No one is in the bathroom. She steps into the entryway and notices the pocket door to the nook her father used as an office is three quarters shut. She slips off her shoes, refills her wine glass, and tiptoes closer to peer inside.

Sure enough, there's Hooley sitting on a futon. When he sees her face in the doorway, he sits up straighter.

"Mrs. Shaw," he says. "Happy New Year."

"Happy New Year, Hooley." She walks inside, then past him, to the window. The glass is cold, but there's still no snow. "Are you hiding? Am I bothering you?"

"Hiding from Pictionary, not from you."

"Oh, me too. I hate Pictionary. I was hiding in the kitchen." Barbara sits next to him on the futon. There's nowhere else to sit. "This room is different."

"I don't think Julie knows what to do with it since your mom passed."

Barbara frowns.

"She used to sleep here," Hooley explains.

Barbara knows this; she merely forgot for a moment. It's disorienting to see her childhood rearranged. The wallpaper has been stripped from the walls in this room. Had it been done by her mother or, more recently, by Julie? "They moved all the bedroom furniture out and stuck this futon in here."

"Strange. This used to be my father's office. He had a roll-top desk there." She points to the far wall. *This is where he died*, she thinks but doesn't say. She looks at the spot on the floor where she tried to resuscitate him while her mother called 911. That her mother chose to sleep here seems odd but practical. It's not as if there's anywhere else.

Someone laughs, and Barbara looks up through the partially opened doorway. There's a straight line to the spot where Julie's sitting, tossing her head back with laughter.

Barbara turns to Hooley and narrows her eyes. "Are you still in love with her?" She surprises herself by blurting out this question. As Hooley's face reddens, she lowers her voice. *It can be our secret.* "Are you?"

He shrugs. "We're better as friends."

Barbara turns to watch Julie leap to her feet and begin acting out her clue. She looks back at Hooley. "That's not the way you're looking at her."

Hooley sighs and takes a swig from his beer. "She's as beautiful now as the day we met. What can I say? She'll always be the one that got away, but at least I have her friendship. She's the best friend I've ever had."

"Julie?"

Hooley laughs, shakes his head. "You don't know her the way I do. You can't. She's too guarded with you."

Barbara nods, feeling scolded. She wonders how much he knows. Wonders if there will be enough time to get to know her daughter unguarded. She tips her head back, drinking the last of her wine, thinking of ways to fill the silence.

"Why did you break up?" She sets her empty wineglass on the floor by her feet and sits back.

Hooley picks at the edge of the label on his beer bottle. "I thought I wanted kids. Seems dumb now, but we were young then."

It's news to Barbara that Julie never wanted children, a determination certain enough that she'd break her own heart. But although Julie had been tight-lipped about the details, Barbara knew she had moved back home because it pained her too much to live in the same state as him. She cried every day for months, walking around with a swollen face and stuffy nose.

"Does she know how you feel?"

Hooley looks up from his beer bottle and smiles. "Don't women always know?"

Barbara scowls. She hadn't known Bill was waiting for her until he sent her a letter when the girls were five. That was the last dinner she cooked for her first husband. She went to bed early with a headache and started packing the next morning, boarding a Greyhound bus with the children while he was at work. She hadn't even left a note. She called Bill from a payphone in Manchester station when she arrived.

Julie appears in the doorway. "Pictionary's over; no more being antisocial!"

They both put up their hands and start to give denials. Julie grabs Hooley's wrist and pulls. She doesn't have to pull hard.

***

As the ball drops, Ruby is asleep on the couch. The married couples kiss, and the rest lift their glasses to one another. Will takes his first sip of champagne.

Barbara leans toward Hooley. "Life's short," she whispers. She's been a widow for longer than she was married. "Tell her."

***

Julie insists on making up the futon herself, as though she's read a book on hostess etiquette. The formality is irritating, treating Barbara as a guest in the house she grew up in.

Barbara leaves the electric candle in the window; the dim glow melts into dawn without allowing sleep in between. She doesn't believe in ghosts, and knows her mother didn't either, but her restlessness must've come from more than the discomfort of the futon. Her mother had slept in this room for years. Had it ever become something other than the room her husband died in?

The conversation had started in the living room. Her mother departed for the kitchen at the word "wedding," shaking her head. Barbara had expected as much but had been naïve enough to think her father could be persuaded. She had followed him to the office, describing the modest ceremony planned for the backyard.

"Because a priest won't marry you in a church," her father said. This stopped her short; of course, he would know. No sense pretending. She'd heard of someone remarrying in the church by getting the first marriage annulled, a long process which made the children bastards, essentially. She certainly didn't think this would make her parents happier. Bill wasn't Catholic either. Truth was, Barbara couldn't say she cared about having a church wedding anyway.

"You already have a husband." Her father sat at his desk with his back to her as if it could project the authority necessary to solve this problem. He turned toward her slightly, looking over his shoulder like she was unworthy of his full attention. "He lives in Ohio and is the father of your children."

Children. He said it with such confidence. Barbara tilted her head, confused. She had always assumed her mother had told him. Her brow furrowed, and his lifted in response.

"The girls," she began, but faltered.

"What about them?"

She swallowed and shifted, trying to make herself taller. "They're Bill's," she said quietly. When he scowled, she thought he hadn't heard. She took a breath, preparing to repeat herself. Instead, she watched as he came to understand.

His face reddened, then went pale. He clawed at his throat, loosening a tie that wasn't there. "Who are you?" he hissed.

"I'm the same person I've always been," Barbara insisted. "I'm your daughter."

He shook his head, looking away from her. He pounded the desktop with his fist, stood, and stumbled toward her, grabbing her roughly by the shoulders.

"Daddy?" Barbara's fear was reflected in his eyes. Her arms went around him, his weight crushing her. Together, they collapsed to their knees. As she helped him lie down on the carpet, she called out for her mother, and her father closed his eyes.

***

Barbara sneaks out of the house before anyone else has woken. There are no other cars on the road, no drivers with New Year's hangovers slowing her down. So, she's surprised, well, disappointed, to find another car in the cemetery parking lot. A hatchback with Virginia plates.

She stops on a whim; she's never been much of a cemetery person. She tries to visit Bill's grave once a year to make sure it looks tidy. She feels responsible. A similar sense of duty makes her stop today. She's rarely in Boothbay. The day is warmer than she expected. Truthfully, she would have preferred bad weather to reflect her mood and ensure she'd have the cemetery to herself. As she makes her way to her mother's grave, she sees the other visitor is near. The figure is huddled close to the spot where Barbara is headed, a young woman with dark hair pulled back tightly against her scalp and arranged into a small ball on top of her head. She's somewhere between eighteen and thirty; Barbara hasn't been able to be any more specific when deciphering ages for decades. As she gets closer, Barbara realizes the girl is standing in front of the exact gravestone where she's headed, and she doesn't know what to do. Walk past her and wait for her to leave or turn around and go back to the car? In the end, she does neither of these things.

Barbara stops a few feet away and clears her throat. The girl looks up, dark eyes wide.

"I didn't mean to startle you. I didn't think there'd be anyone out here this early."

The girl pulls her winter coat closer around her body and says nothing.

"Figured they'd all be hungover." Barbara resents the awkward conversation with herself.

"Hungover?"

"'Cause of New Year's."

"Oh." The girl nods slowly as if this idea requires serious consideration. It occurs to Barbara that she might be high or simply dumb.

"She was my mother." Barbara motions to the headstone.

"Oh! I'm sorry!"

"Thank you." Barbara imagines herself taking the condolence literally. Finally! To be offered an apology for having that woman as a mother, even if it's from someone who has no idea of the facts. "How did you know her?"

The girl hesitates, tips her head, and scowls. "We were friends?" She says this like a question.

Barbara chuckles. "Are you sure?"

The girl seems to take this question more seriously than Barbara intended but smiles. "No, we were."

Barbara nods, relieved she hasn't insulted this stranger.

"I went to the funeral, but I couldn't get up the nerve to talk to you. You look different now; I didn't recognize you."

Barbara touches her hair, confused. "I'm sorry. Do we know each other?"

"Oh, not really. I'm Lisa. We spoke on the phone once."

"We did?"

"Before your mother passed. I was the emergency call person."

Barbara scowls. She remembers the day in September, the call she answered in the car. "But you were friends?"

Lisa smiles crookedly, not making eye contact. She fidgets with her hands in the pockets of her long winter coat. "Once, when she locked herself out of the house, I stayed on the phone until her granddaughter came home to let her in. Afterwards, she called the service to talk sometimes."

"Is that allowed?"

Lisa shrugs. "Not really." She bends, running her fingertips along the top of the gravestone with absent-minded tenderness. "She was a good listener too."

It's hard for Barbara to imagine any of this: her mother as a lonely old woman relying on conversations with strangers; her mother having the kind of interest in others required of a good listener. "The call center is in town?"

"No. It's in Virginia. I came for the funeral, and then I sort of stayed."

"Wow. The funeral was months ago."

"It was a good time for me to go." Lisa smooths her already smooth hair. "Anyway, great to finally meet you. I'll let you have privacy." She lunges forward, giving Barbara a quick and unexpected hug involving mostly shoulder-to-shoulder contact. It's over before Barbara can lift her arms to reciprocate. Or protest.

Barbara calls out goodbye to Lisa's disappearing back. Such an odd girl, living a life without ties to another person, with the freedom to pick up and move at a moment's notice. Barbara tries to think if she's ever felt such freedom. Instead, she'd been creating complicated entanglements with other people since she was a girl. She only felt able to escape one entanglement once she had found herself caught in another.

She turns toward the gravestone, forgetting why she came. To talk to her dead mother? They'd had nothing left to say to each other in life. Dying didn't change that. Besides, Barbara doesn't believe her parents' souls are trapped here anymore than she believes James' soul is trapped in a jar in her closet in Manchester. She likes to imagine all three together somewhere, but she isn't sure she *believes* this, either.

She should have brought the urn, she thinks. If she'd known the day would be warm, she would have. She could bury it right there, and no one would ever have to know. The ground would be getting hard soon, then covered in snow. She'd have to wait for spring.

By the time Barbara gets back to her car, she expects the girl to be gone, but she isn't. She's sitting in the front seat of her car with the driver's door open, one foot in the gravel of the parking lot. As Barbara approaches, Lisa pushes it open more, and Barbara braces herself for another hug.

"Could I get a jump?"

What follows is a morning Barbara hadn't planned for. She moves her car and provides the jumper cables, swallowing her judgment about Lisa not having any. She applies the cables and directs Lisa to try the engine. As she views the car's interior through the gap of the open hood, it becomes clear the car is more than transportation. There's a pillow and blankets making up a bed in the back. Lisa lives here.

"I think you're gonna need a tow," Barbara says finally, and Lisa gasps, her face panic-stricken.

Barbara has always felt competent in an emergency, comfortable taking charge. "It's okay. I know a guy." She pulls out her phone and shoots a text to Hooley. "He won't be up yet. Let me take you to breakfast."

Lisa protests weakly, and Barbara easily gets her way. They drive to a nearby diner opening for business. There's an old man drinking coffee at the counter. He doesn't look up to wish them a happy New Year. They slide into a booth, and Lisa shrugs off her puffy coat, revealing a very pregnant belly.

"Oh!" Barbara can't help but startle. Living in her car *and* pregnant! "How far along are you?" She knows asking this isn't a good idea, in case you're wrong, but Lisa's one of those skinny pregnant women, making it safely obvious.

"Five months."

"Congratulations. My daughter's five months along too." She likes the feeling of saying this to a stranger, as if it's normal. "Do you know if it's a boy or a girl?"

Lisa shakes her head.

"My daughter's the same. Wants to be surprised." Barbara's aware that Liam knows, and Jenna doesn't. They told the story of the ultrasound appointment as if this was charming. "Seems like life is plenty full of surprises," Barbara says as she opens the big, plastic menu.

They sit quietly as they consider their orders. The waitress comes. Barbara gets an omelet; Lisa gets French toast.

"And how about a fruit plate for the table?" Barbara hands over the menu, wondering whether Lisa's been taking prenatal vitamins.

When the waitress leaves, Barbara fidgets with her silverware and paper napkin.

"I'm not keeping it," Lisa says softly, into her lap.

Barbara remembers what they were talking about. "Oh, dear."

Lisa forces a smile. "It's okay. I'd say I wasn't ready, but I'm certainly old enough."

"How old are you?"

"Twenty-six. But I'm not equipped."

"Your parents can't help?"

"I don't know my dad, and I don't really have a relationship with my mom."

"And the baby's father?"

"Not a good guy."

"I'm sorry. It's none of my business."

Lisa shrugs. "It's okay. I found out I was pregnant the day your mom died. I never got to talk to her or get her advice. I sure have made a mess of things figuring it out on my own." She laughs an unconvincing laugh.

When the food comes, they eat quietly. Barbara is pleased to see Lisa shoveling in the food, the fruit too. Her phone buzzes, and she texts Hooley the address and details about the car. She'll pay for the tow and whatever repairs are needed. She'll explain later.

Lisa is mopping up the syrup with her last bite. Barbara sets her phone on the table and considers her approach. Sales is convincing someone you believe in your idea enough for both parties.

"Well, the tow is all set. I think you should come to stay with me while your car is in the shop. I can drive you back when it's fixed."

Lisa looks up, wide-eyed. "Oh, that's nice, but I couldn't."

"Do you have another plan?"

"You don't know me."

This is true. Barbara's kids would think she'd lost her mind, but it's hardly any of their business.

"You were friends with my mom. What else do I need to know?" And then, because Lisa doesn't respond and her lack of confidence makes Barbara feel surer, she leans across the table and grabs her clasped hands. "What do you think she'd tell you to do?"

Chapter Nine

The alarm has been going off for three minutes when Barbara swings her legs out of bed and follows the sound to the bottom of the stairs.

"Rise and shine!" She puts a hand on the banister and waits a moment. Then comes the groan, the slap of flesh on plastic. The alarm stops.

Barbara heads to the kitchen and puts the kettle on before heading to the bathroom to pee. She takes her bathrobe from the hook on the door. Most of the snow has melted by now, but April mornings are still quite chilly.

When Lisa comes into the kitchen, there are two mugs of tea on the table. Barbara has not given up coffee, but she only makes it when Lisa is at work. If she drinks the stuff at Dunkin's, Lisa never says, and Barbara never asks. That's how they are about most things.

There had been no fixing Lisa's car. The repairs would have cost more than the car was worth. Barbara had driven her back to Maine to clean it out. Hooley wrote her a check and claimed he could sell the parts. Then Barbara opened the passenger side door to her sedan and indicated Lisa should get in. They drove back to New Hampshire without ever talking like something had been decided.

In the doorway, Lisa keeps a hand on her back, the Dunkin's uniform stretched tight across her big belly. Jenna would complain the empire waist of the uniform made customers think she was pregnant. There would be no hiding here. Lisa is still so skinny you can see her collarbones. Her belly is huge in comparison, she looks like she might topple over. Monique has done her hair in long braids dangling to her elbows; they remind Barbara of the beaded curtains people used to hang from doorways in the seventies. For work, she keeps them tied in a bundle at the base of her neck.

Once they met her, the kids relaxed. Lisa wasn't someone who took advantage. She spends all day working on her feet and insists on paying rent. Barbara has started a secret bank account to give her after the baby is gone, another thing they never talk about. A social worker came to the house once months ago and asked a few questions about their living situation, their relationship to each other. Barbara could tell she assumed, as her own kids did, this was an act of charity. Barbara didn't view the situation that way, but she isn't exactly sure what it was.

"He was kicking all night," Lisa says, sitting at the table and reaching for her mug.

Barbara's eyebrows lift. "Did you find out the sex?"

Lisa shakes her head. "Oh, no." She lifts the mug and blows across the top. "I say *he*. As a generic." She set the mug down and shrugs. "Maybe I'm sexist."

Barbara shrugs back at her. Too many things are considered sexist these days if you ask her. "Can you eat?"

Lisa shakes her head. Mornings have been hard lately. Barbara had felt sick the whole time she was pregnant with the twins. Back then, she thought God was punishing her, and she deserved it. She doesn't think that anymore. Now she looks back on the young woman she used to be with a lot more kindness. If only we judged our younger selves the way we would as old ladies. She wishes she could articulate this to Lisa, but it's probably something you figure out on your own.

Lisa sits quietly for a while, then sighs heavily at some thought in her own head. She carries the mug to the sink to rinse and set in the dish rack for tomorrow.

They walk through the muddy front yard to the car. There are dirty snow piles at the edge of the road, but the rest has been absorbed by the earth, leaving the ground mushy and uncertain. Barbara walks behind Lisa, ready to grab her if she falls. Last week, Lisa's foot had come loose from her boot, and she'd ended up sitting in a mud puddle. When Barbara rushed to help her up, she looked as if she was crying. She wasn't, though. She was laughing hysterically, contagiously. Barbara had nearly landed in the mud with her.

Later, Lisa said whenever she faced a situation where you must decide whether to laugh or cry, she always laughed. Barbara thinks this worldview of hers is one of the biggest reasons why it's been nice having her around. Since her retirement, Barbara has been bored. And lonely. She liked having someone to talk to, having a routine again.

Most days are like today. Barbara will pull her winter coat over her robe and drive Lisa to work. Then she'll go home, shower, have lunch, watch television or run errands and pick up Ruby from school. They'll get Lisa when her shift ends and hang out until Jenna's workday is over. When they make dinner, Lisa does most of the cooking while Barbara gives directions, sets the table, or chats about her day.

It may seem that she is doing a kindness, but Barbara knows she's getting the better end of the deal.

And sometimes Lisa talks about Barbara's mother. In an offhand, apropos of nothing sort of way. As if she doesn't know what she's saying is often brand-new information, sometimes downright earth-shattering.

***

In the afternoon, it's warm enough to leave their winter jackets in the car. Ruby runs to the swing set while Barbara and Lisa follow at the pace of a woman who's eight months pregnant. The park is fairly empty, and Ruby selects her favorite swing. Lisa takes the one beside her. Ruby digs her toes into the sand, pushing herself as far back as she can, waiting for Barbara to give her a tug and send her sailing forward.

Lisa twists her swing around until she's facing Barbara. "You don't have to pick me up tomorrow. Michael is going to take me car shopping."

"Michael?" Barbara scowls at the unfamiliar name.

"Hooley?"

Barbara's scowl doesn't fade. "I didn't know you two were in touch."

"We text sometimes. I don't know the first thing about buying a car."

Barbara hasn't seen Hooley in months and has no idea whether he followed her advice from New Year's Eve. She has a favorite daydream where he gives her credit in a wedding toast. "Well, I know a little. You could have asked me."

"Oh, I didn't think when he offered. He was coming to town for something else." Lisa shrugs. Barbara wonders if she should tell her about the money she's saved. Would it be smart to use the funds for a new car, or a security deposit whenever Lisa moves out? The truth is, Barbara's afraid to bring up the subject of moving out—for fear she will.

Ruby squeals and leaps from the swing. "Trudy!" Ruby sprints toward the little white dog attached to the familiar older gentleman.

"Shit," Barbara says, and Lisa smiles and turns to see what has inspired the uncharacteristic cursing. She turns back and rearranges her face into one of concern.

Barbara sighs. "It's fine." She has not run into Stewart all winter and had poo-pooed herself for the tiny, in-the-back-of-her-head worry he might be here today: the first slightly warm day of spring. Suddenly, she realizes it's obvious he would be here. He listens to the weatherman, same as she does.

"I'll be right back," Barbara says, throwing her shoulders back as she walks toward her granddaughter.

Stewart is kneeling to Ruby's height as they discuss the dog. He looks up and says hello as Barbara approaches.

"He says I have to check with you," Ruby says.

"Check with me about what?"

"She wants to walk Trudy to the swings."

"He thought Lisa was Mom." Ruby giggles into her shirt sleeve. Barbara looks back to see what he has seen. From this distance, Lisa looks like any pregnant woman.

"Is Trudy up to it?" Barbara bends to stroke the dog's head. She's lying down, her eyes partially closed.

Stewart hands the leash to Ruby. "Go slow."

Ruby jumps up and gives the leash a little tug. Trudy gets to her feet incrementally and walks haltingly. Her decline is obvious and hard to watch.

Barbara turns to Stewart and offers her hand to help him up. He waves her off.

"Has her vision gotten worse?"

He nods. "I was hoping a walk would perk her up. She's been sleeping all day this winter. I'm trying to figure out if she wants to be here."

It takes her a moment to realize he doesn't mean *here*: the park. He means *here*: this mortal coil. "Oh, dear." Barbara motions to the bench, where they sit. It's the same bench where they sat when they used to come to this park together, only a few, short months ago.

Stewart zips his jacket closed, as if feeling a breeze Barbara doesn't. "I wish she could talk to me. It's hard to know what to do."

Barbara nods. "I feel that way about Oliver sometimes. If only they could tell us what they want." Barbara has never witnessed an animal being put to sleep. After Bill died, Jenna assumed the responsibility of taking Norman to the vet when his time came. Barbara hadn't known about it until a week later. "But you've taken such good care of her, given her a really good life."

"Thanks for saying so." Stewart blinks his eyes dry. "I don't mean to burden you with this."

When Barbara had started spending time at Stewart's house, she wondered if Trudy would accept her. Animals can become territorial or jealous, especially as they grow older. But Trudy had always been sweet to her. Not allowed on the furniture, Trudy would lie down on Barbara's feet while she and Stewart sat on the couch in the evening. "Don't be silly. It's no burden."

"Well. It's nice to see you. You're looking—" He struggles to find the right word, and Barbara feels the heat rising to her face. "Happy."

"Oh," she says, relieved.

"Are you seeing anyone?"

The heat returns and she stammers uncomfortably. "No, of course not."

"I assumed that's why you wanted to split up."

"No." She looks away and notices Lisa and Ruby walking toward them with the dog.

"Then, I suppose I'm still confused."

She opens her mouth to speak, but nothing comes out.

"Perhaps I always will be."

"Lisa's gonna puke!" Ruby calls out.

Stewart and Barbara stand. Lisa denies Ruby's allegation, but she looks sufficiently ill, and Barbara determines it's time to go. There are hurried introductions and goodbyes. Barbara bends to stroke Trudy's head and tell her she's a *good girl*. She gives her a scratch under the chin and tries not to think about it being the last time.

***

Ruby falls asleep on the drive home. Lisa leans against the passenger window. "He's stomping on my innards," she mumbles.

"Think of something to keep your mind off it," Barbara suggests.

"Okay." Lisa smiles. Her left hand is pressed to her forehead, covering her eyes. "Who was that guy?"

"Stewart?"

"Ruby said he used to be your boyfriend."

Barbara glances in the rearview mirror. Ruby is asleep in an uncomfortable-looking position. "I'll need to have another talk with her about why it's not nice to gossip."

"What happened?"

"I thought—" Barbara shakes her head. "I might have messed that up."

"Oh, no." Lisa takes her hand off her eyes and reaches out to touch Barbara's arm. "Can you fix it?"

Such a simple question, and Barbara chuckles. Her instinct is to dismiss this as naivety.

***

On Friday nights, they order pizza and watch reality television in the den. Barbara got cable shortly after Lisa moved in. Barbara sits in Bill's chair, and Lisa curls up on the loveseat.

At one of the commercial breaks, Barbara looks over at Lisa. She remembers what it felt like to be pregnant and estranged from her mother. Mothers are supposed to fuss over their pregnant daughters, pass on family histories, teach them how to combat morning sickness and stretch marks.

"Are you sure you can't call your mom?"

Lisa doesn't flinch at the uncharacteristic prying. "I wouldn't have a number to call. Last I heard, she'd got released from jail. I have no idea where she is now."

"Does she know you're pregnant?"

Lisa shakes her head.

"Have you tried to find her? Like, do an internet search for her name or something?"

"A lot of Sue Millers in the world. Besides, shouldn't she be trying to find me? I'm the kid."

"Would you want her to find you?"

"Depends."

"On?"

"Does she only want money?"

Barbara turns back to the television as their show resumes.

At the next commercial break, Lisa picks up the conversation where they left off. "You knew where your mom was your whole life. She never moved. You still never managed to find each other."

"I guess some things in life can't be forgiven."

"What did she do?"

"A million things. She was horrible to me my whole life. But, no, she was the one who couldn't forgive."

"Forgive what?"

"My brother's death."

"James?"

It's startling to hear his name in the mouth of a stranger. "She talked to you about him?"

Lisa nods. "My little brother died when I was three."

"That's awful. How did he die?"

"SIDS. But my mother always blamed herself. I never understood why. Your mom did. She said she felt the same way."

Barbara coughs. "She said she blamed herself?"

Lisa catches the tone of her voice, turns to face her. "Yeah. Because she fell asleep?"

"What do you mean she fell asleep? She wasn't there."

"On the beach?"

"Yes. James and I were on the beach. I left him alone." She'd been hunting for beach glass while he dug in the sand. She wandered too far as the tide came in.

"When you were seven?"

"Eight."

"Alone on the beach with a toddler?"

Barbara pauses. She remembers when her parents first brought James home from the hospital, how she was only allowed to hold him when she sat on the couch with a pillow under her elbow. Her parents were protective of him. As he learned to walk, they kept all the doors locked to keep him from toddling outside. They understood how treacherous the ocean could be. Would her mother have let her take James down to the water's edge on her own?

But this is how she remembers it. It's been this way in her head all these years, with a clarity a would be impossible to invent. She can still hear her mother's scream. She'd come down from the house to check on them and found James, face down in a tidepool. She'd been holding him to her chest, screaming a high-pitched, blood-curdling scream as Barbara ran home.

Why would she lie about it?

"She said she fell asleep?"

Lisa nods.

***

After she drops Lisa off at work on Saturday, Barbara has nothing on her schedule. She goes home and takes a long, hot shower, then sits in her kitchen to write a grocery list.

Ground turkey, white beans, enchilada sauce, cilantro. Lisa wants to learn how to make green chili.

She gets into her car and makes a series of turns as if she's going to the grocery store. But then she takes a right instead of a left and ends up parked outside Stewart's house. She sits in the car for quite a while, thinking about what she might say. She contemplates driving away, but this seems considerably more pathetic. What is she afraid of? Barbara has never been the sort of woman to chase after a man. Even her first husband had done the chasing, though the pursuit didn't take him long, and he stopped chasing soon after he caught her. He was the first man to ever tell her she was beautiful, and she remembers thinking he might be the only man in the world who would ever think so.

Her Bill had chased her from the beginning, from the beach in Maine to her isolation in Ohio to their eventual, happy life together. He chased her in little ways every day, and she let herself be caught over and over. She never would have sent him a letter like the one he sent her, full of hopeful desperation. And she knows without the letter, they never would have had their happy life.

In the end, she rings the bell and watches through the kitchen window as Stewart turns, sees her, and looks confused. He's wiping his hands on a dishtowel as he opens the door. He says nothing.

Barbara shrugs. "Hi," she says. It's not one of the greetings she practiced.

"Hi," he says back.

"Can I come in?"

"Of course," he says, stepping back and opening the door wider. "I was making a grilled cheese. Would you like one?"

Barbara smells the butter heating in the pan. She's forgotten to have lunch. "Oh, I don't want to be any trouble."

"It's no trouble." He gets two more slices of bread out of the bag.

Barbara pulls out a barstool and sets her purse on the counter. She watches him carve the Havarti on the cutting board. He passes her one of the slices and she pops it in her mouth.

She chews and swallows. She wishes she had something to drink. "We didn't get to finish our conversation from yesterday."

"No. I suppose we didn't." He gets two glasses from the cupboard. "Was your friend okay?"

"Oh, yes. Just pregnant."

He opens the refrigerator and begins to list beverage options. She suggests they split a soda, something they used to do all the time, neither of them needing a full can. Barbara likes carbonation, but too much gives her the hiccups.

Stewart snaps the can open, hands it to her, and goes back to the sandwiches. She fills their glasses evenly. He gets the plates out; she reaches for napkins from a porcelain napkin holder. The sandwiches sizzle in the pan and the smell of melted cheese fills the room. Barbara wishes they could stay in this moment.

Once he has plated each sandwich, Stewart moves to the other side of the counter and takes the stool next to her.

They eat, and she compliments the chef. At first, keeping her mouth full avoids an awkward moment. She tries to get her thoughts together, aware of her own chewing, swallowing. She's eating too fast.

Barbara takes a few breaths as the comfortable silence tips into something else. "I realized after I saw you yesterday, I left things unclear."

Stewart takes a bite of his grilled cheese, committing nothing.

"I've never been good at putting all my cards on the table."

Stewart chuckles. "Ah," he says. "An understatement."

Barbara feels like he's laughing at her, which rankles her. She picks up the sandwich and tries to remember what she came to say. "I think we're quite different people." She's looking at her plate in front of her, but she can see from the corner of her eye he's nodding. "I remember something you said to me about how I lie about things that don't matter."

He stops nodding. "I'm sorry."

"No, I think you're right. You never lie."

"It's part of my recovery."

Barbara nods and takes a sip of her soda. "I have a more flexible relationship with the truth."

"Flexible." Stewart lifts a dubious eyebrow, but Barbara is adamant.

"For one thing, not everyone is owed the absolute truth. People are rude and nosy. And, for a long time in my life, lying was survival for me." She thinks about life with her first husband, lying about her eating habits and her weight, lying about what she prayed for or whether she'd prayed at all, lying about talking to the mail man or why the gas tank was lower than expected. "And I got used to it. And I felt people wouldn't like me without some embellishment. I'm not saying it's okay, but not many people know me without lies—maybe only Bill did. You might not like the truth of me."

"Well, I suppose that's the risk."

They eat quietly for a while. Barbara thinks she might finish the sandwich, thank him, and go. The rest feels too hard.

"I wanted to apologize."

"For?"

"For being unclear."

He sighs, eats his last bite and stacks their empty plates. "An apology isn't helpful if you aren't going to at least try to explain yourself."

"Oh." She's never heard this kind of sharpness in his voice. She thinks of all the apologies she has refused to offer when owed, how surprised Jenna would be if she could see this attempt to give one at all. But that's not what Stewart wants.

The plates crash into the sink. "You said we wanted different things, but you never asked me what I wanted," he says.

"I know. I made that up. That wasn't why."

He groans and covers his face with his hands.

"I have this thing I do where if I think you're going to reject me, I reject you first."

"But I wasn't going to reject you."

"I started to understand that when I saw you yesterday."

He comes around the counter and sits next to her again, taking her hands. "You are the first person I've let into my heart since Rita died."

Barbara drops her head, unable to look him in the eye. She wishes she had been more worthy of the distinction. But then she takes notice of the tense he has used.

"Am I still there?" she asks, pressing her palm to his chest.

He answers by kissing her passionately. His hands are in her hair. She fingers the buttons of his shirt. He pulls away. "Neither of us have time to waste on these kinds of games."

She nods, and he pulls her close again, this time his lips are on her neck, and his hands grip her thighs. "I missed this," she whispers, and he grunts in agreement, stands up, and leads her quickly down the hall.

Chapter Ten

Stewart usually meets his dad for breakfast on Sunday mornings, and Barbara sleeps in and texts Monique around nine.

Brunch?

She finds Trudy asleep in her dog bed in the living room. She sits cross-legged on the carpet in front of her, unsure if she should wake her up. Asleep, the dog looks content, but how would she know? Her phone buzzes in her back pocket, and Trudy opens her eyes by half. She wags her tail twice, then closes her eyes again. She does not appear significantly surprised to see her there.

Barbara looks at her phone.

Want me to swing by and pick you up?

Barbara runs her hands through Trudy's curls and gets to her feet.

She writes back: *I'm on the east side. Meet at Berty's?*

Monique is at a table near the front of the restaurant when Barbara comes in.

"Where are you coming from?"

Barbara hangs her purse on the back of a chair and sits down. "Stewart's."

"Oh, my! Tell me everything!" The waitress comes to give them coffee, and they wave away the offered menu. They're regulars, here for their usual: fried eggs, hash browns, bacon, and toast.

"We had a talk last night," Barbara says.

"Last night?" Monique sits back in her chair, pretends to look at a wristwatch she isn't wearing. "Must have been a real good talk!"

Barbara smiles. Monique is the first real girlfriend she's ever had. Growing up, she'd been solitary. She'd never been to a sleepover and couldn't have invited anyone to her house. Her mother slept most days, waking in time to make dinner for her unsuspecting husband. In high school, Barbara fell in with the girls who smoked and had a certain reputation. Long enough to attract her first husband, who moved her away from everyone she knew and was wary of her forming any new connections. By the time she regained the freedom to do it, she'd forgotten how. If she'd ever known. Other women never seemed to like her. She was a working mom before it was acceptable. And by the time it became the norm, she was the boss.

But Monique was the boss in her life, a single mother running her own business. Barbara didn't have anything to intimidate Monique. They understood each other right away.

"So, are you back together?" Monique asks.

"He didn't exactly say that."

"But you spent the night?"

Barbara's lips twitch into a smile Monique takes as an answer. "I think he's somewhat guarded."

Monique nods. "Fair enough."

Barbara scowls.

"Well, you did end things rather abruptly. I never quite understood what he did wrong."

"He didn't really do anything wrong. It's more like—" Barbara's eyes skitter around the room as she searches for a platitude. "We had a miscommunication."

The food comes and they help the waitress make room on the table. Then they're quiet as they eat. Monique doesn't press for a better explanation.

"What does he think about the stray you've taken in?"

"It didn't come up."

Monique presses a corner of toast against the shining yolk of her egg, coloring the plate yellow. "What are her plans after she has the baby?"

"We haven't discussed that yet."

"Aren't you cutting this close? She's going to have the baby any minute now." She mops up yolk with toast, chews.

"I don't want her to think I'm itching for her to move out."

Monique looks up from her plate, holding the last bite of toast aloft. "Ever?"

Barbara reaches for her coffee. "When she's ready, whether she's had the baby or not." She lifts the mug. "That's not why she's here."

"No?"

"Not the only reason. I like her. Don't you like her?" She sets the mug down on the table, loudly.

"I do. I also like all my own kids, but I expected them to move out when they're grown."

Barbara lifts her mug again and drinks slowly. It's so hot, it's almost painful. "She has no one. She doesn't know where her mother is."

"How is that possible? This day and age?"

Barbara shrugs. What had Lisa said? "Apparently, she has a very common name."

Monique shakes her head in dismissal. "Give me the name. I'll have Eric do a search." Eric is her son, a computer programmer. "He can find anyone. Virginia, right?

"Well, who knows if she's still there. Lisa said she was in jail for a while." She whispers the word *jail*, in case anyone is eavesdropping.

"In jail for what?"

"I didn't ask."

Monique rolls her eyes. She opens the notes app and slides her phone across the table. "Type in her name. And any other details you know. Give me twenty-four hours."

After they've finished eating, the plates are cleared away, and they wait for the bill.

"Are you ready for the party?" Monique asks.

The twins are turning forty on Friday. Jenna is too pregnant to drive to Boothbay or host a party, so Barbara volunteered. She can't remember the last birthday party she'd thrown for them in tandem, before Julie had been held back in school, and they had different sets of friends and demanded everything separate.

"I was thinking we could play Pin the Tail on the Donkey."

"No Musical Chairs. Jenna would kill you."

"Yes, I expect Jenna to sit in the same chair all night. The baby is due next week, but Ruby and Will were both early."

"Are you ready for *that*?"

Barbara sighs. She's been feigning acceptance for a while now, but she hasn't quite given up hope. Months ago, she had offered to foot the bill for an egg donor. Jenna explained it wasn't only about the prohibitive cost but the exploitation of financially desperate people—for much the same reason you can't buy a kidney off the black market but can get one donated by a loved one. Barbara managed not to point out how in Jenna's utopia, the financially desperate person stays financially desperate.

Since then, Barbara's had another idea and is struggling to figure out the right way to propose it. She thinks the party might be the perfect time and place. Now or never. She can't ask Monique, though.

"It is what it is," she says instead. Such an idiotic platitude.

***

As Barbara pulls into her driveway, a beat-up red truck is pulling out. Hooley smiles and waves when he sees her, but he doesn't stop to chat or explain why he was there. There's another car in the driveway: a royal blue Honda sedan with paper license plates. Barbara thinks it's possible Lisa went to bed early and didn't know yet she'd been gone overnight. She didn't think to call.

Lisa is standing in front of the refrigerator when Barbara comes in, wearing her pajamas. This strikes Barbara as odd, but she doesn't say it.

"Looks like car shopping was a success," she says instead, setting her purse on the table.

Lisa grins. "Isn't it cute? Michael made sure we got a good deal, and the car has all the responsible safety stuff." She walks to the window over the sink and looks out. "It's the same color as my high school prom dress. I love it."

Barbara pulls out a kitchen chair and sits down. "Did you have to go back over to the car dealership this morning?" This couldn't explain Lisa's pajamas, but she doesn't know how to make sense of Hooley in her house the morning *after* the car shopping. She can't ask directly, and it's rude to assume. Lisa still hasn't asked her where she was last night.

"No." Lisa frowns, confused, then seems to understand. "He ended up staying over. We were up late talking, and it's such a long drive. I didn't think you'd mind."

"I don't." Barbara shrugs. Is Hooley the kind of man who'd go after a pregnant woman? She doesn't know him very well. "I worry about you."

Another frown. Lisa leans against the counter with her arms crossed over her belly. "Worry about me?" Then her eyes bulge. "Barbara! He slept in the room across the hall."

"Jenna's room?" She feels relieved for reasons she doesn't understand.

"Of course. Did you think he slept with *me*?" She stands up straighter and reties the belt on her robe. "I mean, it's a compliment you think I'm capable. I feel about as sexy as—" She pauses and looks down at herself. "A bean bag chair."

Barbara laughs. "You're beautiful, pregnant or not."

Does she think Hooley is spoken for? That, in a sense, he belongs to Julie? Maybe, partly. But there's something more. Barbara doesn't want to see Lisa getting tied to a man right as she is about to be free.

"You're the one who stayed out all night. Projecting." Lisa sits across the table from her, smiling, her eyes narrowed.

Barbara can't help herself from the fleeting thought: *Is Lisa a good liar too?* She shakes it off.

"You gave me some good advice in the car yesterday."

"I did? I don't remember giving you advice."

"Maybe you didn't mean to, but you asked if I thought I could fix things with Stewart. And I've been thinking."

"Oh!" Lisa reaches for her hand across the table. "I'm glad."

Barbara slowly realizes: Hooley knows she didn't come home last night. Will he tell Julie? She can't believe she has to worry about such things at her age.

***

Barbara wakes from a version of the same dream she's had every night since her talk with Lisa about James. It always ends the same way, with the screaming. Tonight, the dream started tranquil enough: her young mother in sunglasses, lying on a blanket, reading a magazine. She's beautiful, buxom, her dark curls loose around her shoulders. The blanket is a blue plaid with fringe edges, rough beneath Barbara's palms. James is sitting in the sand with his back to them, digging with his yellow shovel, filling the pail.

"Beautiful day," her mother murmurs, and then she is asleep; the magazine falls open across her midsection.

Barbara gets to her feet and backs away slowly. James looks back at her, and she holds a finger to her lips. He grins and gets back to work. That pail isn't going to fill itself.

The ocean is dark blue; small waves are topped with white froth. As she walks away, the sand gets firmer, wetter. The first piece of glass is large and green—once a beer bottle, but the ocean has worn away its sharp edges. Not special enough to keep, she drops it.

There are others she does keep. There is a pale green and a lavender one so small, it disappears under her thumb. She keeps them in the square pocket of her sundress, feeling the weight of them as they click together. The curve of the beach ahead of her grows slimmer as the tide comes in. Maybe it's time to head back.

And that's when she hears the screaming and wakes up.

***

It doesn't take Monique twenty-four hours, and she doesn't need to enlist her son for help. Barbara finds an email in her inbox Monday morning. Subject: Sue Miller. The body of the email contains only the blue link. Barbara spends the next hour learning about this woman, this blond mother of three blond boys who play soccer and look like their dad.

On her *About* page, Sue mentions her daughter, Lisa, whose name does not show up as a blue link because Lisa does not have a Facebook account.

Barbara joined years ago and hardly ever logs in anymore. At the beginning, she friended all the girls she knew in high school long enough to look at their photos, determine which ones had gotten fat, and then unfriend them. It seemed they'd all gotten fat, while the girls who had been considered fat when they were in school looked like average-sized women.

Initially, Barbara thinks she should give this link to Lisa, but quickly determines how stupid that would be. There is no way Lisa doesn't have this information. Sue Miller is not in hiding. She's posing her sons for first-day-of-school photos on the front stoop of a grand, white house with brass numbers on a red door. And while it might be offensive to say Sue doesn't look like a woman who's been to prison, there's no notable chunk of time when she hasn't been posting pictures of birthday parties or inspirational quotes about God.

Barbara finds herself fascinated by this woman. Sue Miller is considerably younger than her, by more than a decade, at least. Her best guess is the boys are about five, seven, and nine. The photos she posts of her children, and often several of their friends, are of these adventurous outings to the zoo or an apple orchard or a museum. Sue Miller seems to delight in this role as the neighborhood Mother Goose.

Barbara remembers getting roped into chaperoning one of Jenna's field trips. She generally used work as an excuse, but she'd been going through a phase, trying harder. She had to sit in the front of the bus next to Marsha Healey, who had endless stories about her children, her dogs, the agonizing decision she was making over wallpaper patterns. Marsha didn't work outside the home, and she was part of a growing contingent of suburban white women who agreed whole-heartedly stay-at-home moms have the hardest job on Earth. This was back before you could tune someone out by gazing at your cellular phone. On the trip back, Barbara had feigned motion sickness to get some peace and quiet. A day of screeching eight-year-olds topped by a sanctimonious PTA mom was too much to take.

Lisa drove herself to work this morning, and Barbara hasn't seen her all day. At first, the realization she's been lied to feels like a hot poker in the middle of her chest. She feels self-righteous: after she'd opened her home to this needy stranger! Then comes the woozy wave of embarrassment. Barbara feels her face flush and sweat. What would people think? She imagines confronting Lisa when she gets home, throwing her out.

But that isn't what she wants.

***

Jenna's last client cancels, and Barbara brings Ruby straight home after school. She's quiet in the back seat, thinking her own five-year-old thoughts, leaving Barbara to reconstruct Lisa's life, adding this new knowledge to what she's been told, understanding only parts are true.

Had Lisa ever known her father? Had he left them after her brother's death? Based on the apparent ages of her mother's new children, she would have remarried when Lisa was in high school. Following some years as a struggling single mother, she'd been rescued by a wealthy white man. Had he been kind to Lisa? Threatened? Predatory? They would have moved into his big house, where her mother no longer needed to work at anything besides giving him sons and luxuriating in motherhood as she never could before. Her mother's fabulous new life would have started about the time Lisa was coming of age, moving out on her own. Was this when they had become estranged?

Jenna meets them at the door. She gets Ruby settled at the kitchen table, where they begin negotiations about snacks. Jenna tries to sell peanut butter on celery; Ruby wants Oreos. They settle on two Oreos, a granola bar, and a juice box.

Jenna sets the food on the table across from her daughter. "Where's Lisa?"

"She bought a new car and doesn't need me anymore." Barbara's laughter is forced, but Jenna doesn't seem to notice.

"Good for her. Will she get her own place once the baby's born?"

"Why do people keep asking that?"

"I thought you were helping her get back on her feet. It's been months. She has a steady job and a car. She's doing better."

"Yes, she is. But do you think once she gives her baby away would be the best time to kick her out?"

"I didn't say kick her out. God. I thought that was the point. No?"

Barbara shrugs. She's not sure she could articulate the point if she ever had one. Certainly not today.

"I have a book for her." Jenna gets to her feet slowly. "We talked about it last week."

Barbara follows Jenna into her office with the floor to ceiling bookcases. Freud, *Reviving Ophelia*, *The Emotionally Absent Mother*. There's a pile of books on her desk, and Jenna sorts them until she finds the right one.

"It's about breathing techniques during childbirth."

"Don't you need it?" Barbara asks. "You're due before she is."

Jenna shakes her head. "I've committed the main facts to memory. Tell her the most important parts are highlighted."

Barbara takes the book. It's hard to imagine the two women having this conversation. Where was she?

Both enormously pregnant women are giving their babies away, yet their circumstances are not at all the same. Jenna would probably have something to say about Lisa's deception, some psychological insight. Barbara isn't sure if it's embarrassment or a sense of loyalty that makes her keep it to herself.

Barbara doesn't spend much time wondering about the why of it. She knows quite well there are lies that can feel quite true, for many reasons. Maybe Lisa's mother hadn't abandoned her for a life of crime and addiction, but that's how it felt. Maybe this would have been easier to understand or explain to nosy strangers, discouraging follow-up questions.

***

When Lisa comes home from work, Barbara is sitting at the kitchen table.

"Is everything okay?" Lisa asks before she shuts the door.

Barbara clears her throat and looks away, tries to rearrange her facial expression from whatever Lisa has seen. Not everyone deserves the absolute truth, she remembers telling Stewart.

"Everything's fine." She smiles. "How was your day?"

Lisa sits at the table, rubbing her belly, looking uncertain. "Okay."

And what right does Barbara have to indignation? What has she done to earn Lisa's trust? What does this girl owe her?

"If I've overstayed my welcome, I can be out in a day or two," Lisa says.

Barbara gasps and shakes her head. "Don't be silly," she says quickly.

Barbara is overwhelmed by a feeling she can't quite identify. Not pity, exactly, though she does feel sorry for this motherless, pregnant girl, even knowing some of her circumstances were the results of her own choices. Barbara understands and feels defensive. Barbara wants to protect Lisa from herself in all the ways she wishes someone had protected her.

Lisa sighs and sits back in the chair. "You look serious."

Barbara decides not to tell what she knows. If Lisa finds comfort in her secrets, who is Barbara to take that from her?

"I was sitting here, thinking." Barbara speaks slowly, inventing as she goes. What might she have been thinking? "About the baby."

Lisa's eyes widen, as if this takes her by surprise, but she nods.

"Are you ready?"

She takes a deep breath, blows it out, and shrugs. Barbara remembers who she was when they met: the pregnant girl living in her car without jumper cables. Three months later, she's still unprepared.

This feeling is new for Barbara. A warm heaviness in her chest. Has she ever felt this for her own children? Those lucky kids have never known true hardship, true loss. If she had felt something like this, it was for herself.

"Your due date is rapidly approaching." Barbara hasn't planned this, but the conversation she'd planned is all wrong. She remembers the book in her purse, stands to retrieve it, and places it on the table. "From Jenna."

Lisa opens the book and thumbs through it, absently.

"I was surprised, to be honest." Barbara sits back down. "You never talk to me about the birth."

Lisa shrugs. "You never ask."

Barbara supposes this is true. She had thought she was respecting Lisa's privacy. "Well, you can," she says. "Talk to me." And then, because it's been on her mind, she asks: "Have you ever thought about an open adoption?"

Lisa frowns. "Is this where you go to the kid's birthday party each year, and everyone wonders how you could be so damaged that you'd give him up?"

"Oh, well, that sounds awful. No. The arrangement can be set up in different ways, however you want. Like photos or letters back and forth or being available if he wants to have a chat when he turns twelve. I don't know. Depends on the parents and how much anonymity everyone wants. Maybe with all the DNA and social media these days, that's impossible. I suppose this is sort of what we have with Ruby. Families are made up all sorts of ways, and it doesn't have to be awful."

Lisa is quiet, chewing her bottom lip and staring at her hands. Barbara feels her building up the nerve to say something. She waits.

"You don't think I'm a horrible person?" Lisa asks, her voice small and scratchy.

"Of course not." Barbara's answer is immediate. "I think giving up a child to provide a better life must be the hardest, kindest thing a person can do."

She hears the words as she says them, and she means them, but she knows they'd sound different to Jenna. Hypocritical or completely false. She shakes away the thought. "Maybe you can talk to Liam about it. He'll be at the party. Just an idea." She tries to make this sound casual and unrehearsed, but she isn't sure she succeeds. She stands then, clears her throat. "It's getting dark out. We should start thinking about dinner."

***

Barbara could have corrected the lie more easily when the girls were small, before they could be angry, before they were old enough to get into a car and drive away.

For months before the wedding, she and Bill had argued every night. Once the truth had killed her father, it was no longer up for discussion. The secret would be a condition of their marriage. Bill would have agreed to anything by then. He had a son from his second marriage he never saw. His daughters would see him every day, would take him for granted. He'd tuck them in and kiss their boo-boos and help with their homework. What did it matter what they called him?

Nothing in their lives would have been any different. Barbara told herself this at the time, and the girls, later. He had been their father in every way that counted. Knowing the truth might have saved Jenna and Julie from the weeks in Ohio during the summer; Barbara couldn't think of a reason to keep them home.

Jenna thinks it's particularly perverse Barbara referred to her first husband as the *biological*, but that's what he was: Billy's biological father. Barbara had said this dismissively; aside from those two weeks a year, no one ever heard from him. The nickname stuck. This way, he was easier to distinguish from the other Bills in her life.

It wasn't exactly a lie though—more like she didn't correct a false assumption. She has learned to keep this distinction to herself. It did not go over well.

While she was trapped in her first marriage, it didn't feel like a lie. It was something that had to be true for her own safety, to keep her from being thrown out on the street with her babies, from losing custody of her son. And so, it was true. Eventually, she came to believe it.

During her second marriage, the secret was hers and hers alone. She didn't think of her daughters as people entitled to know the story of where they came from. They were children. The story belonged to her as much as they did. After the wedding, Bill never brought it up again. He had lost the battle but won much more. He had everything he'd ever wanted.

Chapter Eleven

Barbara enters Party City and puts a red basket over her arm. She considers this an arrogant move, assuming she will find everything she's looking for. Usually, she doesn't get a basket until she has managed to find too much to carry.

For years, the girls insisted on themes. Julie liked Disney princesses and *My Little Pony*; Jenna liked *Ghost Busters* and *Goonies* and *Super Mario Brothers*. Barbara begins by choosing the paper plates. She will build the color scheme around it: streamers and balloons and cone hats and noise makers. She doesn't recognize any of the cartoon characters represented here. Perhaps she should have brought Ruby along.

As she wavers between the unicorn or butterfly plates, Barbara can't help wondering how their lives might have been different if she had never separated the girls in school. Such a small thing at the time. The young teacher had insisted that Jenna's overprotection would stunt Julie's social growth. And Barbara had assumed a college degree and a few years presiding over first graders made this woman an expert.

As babies and toddlers, the girls had babbled their own secret language to each other. She remembers feeling jealous of their closeness, which changed almost immediately when Jenna started second grade and Julie stayed back. Suddenly, for the first time in their lives, they were spending most of their days apart. They had different homework, different friends. When Jenna started junior high, they rode different school buses to different schools. Julie *had* grown more independent, more social, but maybe that would have happened in time anyway. And what was the cost?

What do they call it? When changing one thing ends up causing a series of changes? The butterfly effect. No way of knowing what one small thing would have changed. The sisters might live next door to each other, raising children close in age, never thinking about giving one of them away.

Barbara selects the butterfly plates and is filling the red basket with matching cups and napkins as her phone begins to ring. She sets the basket down to rummage through her purse. By the time she sees Stewart's number, it's already been ringing for too long.

"Hello!" she shouts, afraid to miss the call she's been pretending not to wait for.

It's quiet on the other end, but she can hear him breathing.

"Stewart?"

Barbara's stomach flip-flops. Is he nervous? Has he changed his mind? Is he calling to break things off?

She thinks about hanging up. She might prefer to be ghosted than to hear all the reasons she is not a good risk.

He coughs and takes a deep breath in, snottily. "I'm sorry," he chokes. He's crying.

"Stewart, what's wrong?" In the ensuing silence, she feels a whole different kind of panic. A car wreck. A cancer diagnosis. His father's death.

"It's Trudy," he manages, and she feels relieved, even as her heart is breaking.

"Where are you?" She hoists her purse strap over her shoulder and heads for the exit, leaving the red basket on the floor behind her. "I'm coming."

***

There's a young woman in the waiting room with a pet carrier on her lap. Her blond ponytail is coming loose as she whispers soothing words through the locked door and is answered by the low growl of an animal much larger than the carrier should be able to contain. Barbara remembers how Oliver had hated going to the vet as a kitten. Once, she'd had to catch him in a pillowcase, then zip him up in a duffle bag and hope he didn't suffocate on the drive over. Another time, she'd had to call and cancel because she couldn't catch him. As he got older, he got easier to catch but harder to persuade out of the carrier once they were in the vet's office. He'd plaster himself against the end farthest from the door and resist all bribes.

Barbara stands at the front desk and gives her name to an older woman with spikey gray hair.

"I'm here for Stewart."

The woman's face falls, and she gets to her feet, hurriedly. "Of course," she says, and she steps out from behind the counter. "Come with me." She leads Barbara down a hallway to the last door on the left.

Inside, Trudy is asleep on the examining table, and Stewart is standing beside her. There are two empty chairs in the corner. Stewart looks up as Barbara steps inside.

"Take all the time you need," says the woman from the front desk, pulling the door closed before anyone can be expected to respond.

He reaches for her hand while he continues patting Trudy. "Thanks for coming."

"Of course."

"I thought I was fine. I was halfway here, bawling my eyes out in the car before I realized I shouldn't be driving."

Barbara isn't used to men who cry—never mind men who talk about crying without shame. "I'm glad you called me." She lets go of his hand and steps closer to rub his back. He's so tall. She slides her hand up and down his spine, slowly, mimicking the way he moves his hand through Trudy's fur.

He bends close to the dog's face. "I love you a bushel and a peck, a bushel and a peck and a hug around the neck." His voice is quiet and raspy, cracking on the last word. "Rita used to sing that. At least she'll be with Rita now."

"That's a nice thought," she says. And it is. If only she believed in such things, she might see Bill again or have a chance to ask her mother all the questions she'd never known to wonder about.

"The doctor said to take my time, but now that it's been decided, I don't want to drag it out. I don't want to put her through another minute."

"I understand," Barbara says.

Stewart knocks on the door to the back room to signal his readiness. Barbara caresses Trudy's curls and bends to kiss her nose. The dog's eyes flutter open and close again.

The vet comes in with a somber face, and things start to move quickly. There are two shots close together, and Trudy seems to deflate like a Christmas lawn decoration. Her head grows heavier; her breaths come further apart.

Stewart stands with his hand resting gently on her back the whole time.

"She's gone," the vet says. He reiterates there's no rush and disappears out the door.

It was both faster and more peaceful than Barbara had expected. She'd like to imagine a similar send-off when it's her time: drifting off painlessly while her favorite song is whispered in her ear by someone she loves. What would they choose? "Isn't She Lovely," or "Here Comes the Sun."

Stewart turns to her. "Can we leave?"

"If you're ready."

He nods. "Suddenly, I'm tired."

"You've done everything she needed."

He lets her lead him to her car. When she moves to fasten his seat belt, he stops her gently, touching her face. "I'm okay."

He's quiet on the drive, his head tipped back, eyes closed. Barbara can't be sure he's awake until she pulls into his driveway, and he sits up.

"Can you come in?"

Barbara looks at the clock on the dashboard. "Ruby will be out soon." She's getting used to a new schedule, no longer picking Lisa up from work, taking Ruby to the park by herself. "I'm sorry."

"It's fine. I'll probably lie down."

"I can come back," she offers, hopefully. "Bring dinner?"

He smiles. "That sounds great."

***

In the morning, Barbara wakes up in Stewart's bed and helps him collect Trudy's little toys throughout the house. The squeaky, rubber pig, the tennis ball she brought back after one throw, the threadbare, plush lion that had lost its stuffing years before.

After a leisurely breakfast, she drives Stewart to pick up his car, and they make plans for the following night. When she gets home, Barbara finds Oliver curled in a ball on her bed. Usually, she would tiptoe around him, but today, she pulls him against her body as she lies down and nuzzles into the soft fur of his neck. He protests mildly, opening his mouth in a wide yawn and letting out a squeak before curling up into a new ball under her hand.

***

Julie arrives Friday afternoon to help Barbara set up for the party. She empties the bags from Party City onto the kitchen table. Ruby had chosen the unicorn plates, making the color scheme purple and turquoise.

Julie fingers the crepe paper of the streamers. "Pretty retro, huh?"

"I got Pin the Tail on the Donkey too."

"I don't think kids play that anymore. Everything is high tech."

"Low tech used to be fine. When you were babies, you'd play with my pots and pans for hours. Now everyone's giving screens to their newborns."

"Hell in a handbasket." Julie shakes her head with mock concern.

Barbara sits at the table to blow up the balloons as Julie stands on a chair to tape the first end of the streamers. "Is Hooley coming? I expected you'd drive up together."

"He's coming. It's too long a drive."

Barbara scrunches her face. "Isn't this exactly why you'd do the drive together?"

Julie sighs. "Things are too awkward right now for a three-hour car ride." She shrugs. "It'll blow over. We've been through worse."

"What happened?"

Barbara waits for the inevitable signal to back off. It's personal. It's a long story. It's none of her business. Instead, Julie steps down from the chair and sits at the table. "He told me he's still in love with me. That he's always been in love with me."

"Oh?"

"This was months ago."

"And it's not a good thing?"

Julies glares at her. "No! It's not a good thing. He's my best friend, but we were never good for each other in that way. We wanted different things. We still do."

"Kids?"

Julie looks at her quizzically. "Yes."

"You've never wanted them?"

"Never."

"Well, maybe he changed his mind. This was—what? Fifteen years ago? And he never found anyone else to have kids with."

"The thing is, he hasn't changed. And that ship has sailed for me—I mean, I'm glad. Less pressure. But he still has time."

"You have time. Look at Jenna."

She slaps the table. "You're not listening. I don't *want* to."

Barbara raises her hands in surrender, bites her tongue.

"Everyone assumes all women want to be mothers, and there's something wrong with you if you don't. But I never have."

Barbara can't remember wanting children or not wanting children. She already had them before she'd had time to give it much thought.

"I don't think there's anything wrong with you."

Julie narrows her eyes, skeptically. "You don't?"

"No."

"Well, that's nice to hear." She stands and chooses a purple balloon to tape at the corner above her head. "I married Rick 'cause he didn't want kids. But that wasn't enough."

"I suppose not." Encouraged by her uncharacteristic sharing, Barbara presses for more. "Are you seeing anyone these days?"

Julie loops the streamers and stretches her arm, lifting one foot. Barbara is afraid the chair will tip, but she's more afraid to say so. Julie smiles crookedly. "Maybe."

Before she can say more, Monique arrives with the cake, and Lisa comes downstairs to make her *famous* three bean salad. By the time Jenna and Sam arrive with the kids, the decorations have been hung and everyone is wearing a cone-shaped hat with an elastic under their chin.

It reminds Barbara of the last birthday party they'd had for Bill. He'd been turning sixty-eight. On an unseasonably warm day in October, they carried his recliner out into the back yard. Only family was there: the girls, his son and daughter-in-law, his grandson. And Sam. Bill had insisted on inviting him, though he and Jenna were newly dating then.

When Liam and Marco ring the bell, Ruby's blindfolded for her turn at the donkey. Jenna waves hello from the recliner in the corner, and Barbara hands them a unicorn plate full of crackers and bean salad to bring her.

Everyone laughs when Ruby pins the tail to the donkey's nose. Monique tells a tragic story about a gender reveal party that ended in a forest fire. It seems like odd timing for a trend about revealing gender. With all the people screaming about whether to let trans kids change in the locker room of their choice, Barbara thinks a simpler, much more important question is being ignored: Why are we still forcing children to get naked in front of each other?

Barbara remembers the embarrassment of changing in front of other girls in high school when all she had was an undershirt. Her mother hadn't believed in training bras. You didn't get a bra until you needed one, and Barbara didn't need one. When she finally did, the relief of locker-room shame was the first boon.

She didn't blossom until her junior year, at which point her breasts got her invited to parties she'd never known existed.

Hooley gets to the party in time for cake and ice cream. He sits at the kitchen table with Lisa while Julie eats hers in the living room.

Barbara pulls Liam aside. "I was hoping you might get a chance to talk to Lisa."

"Oh?" He's standing by the refrigerator, holding a plateful of cake in his left hand, the fork in his right.

"She's interested in open adoption, and I know what you have with Ruby isn't exactly that, but I thought you might be able to speak to the openness of it. Reassure her that the process can be normal, welcoming, and good."

He smiles. "When is she due?"

"Oh, very soon. Weeks." She pretends to catch eyes with Monique, excusing herself to find out what she needs. She doesn't dare push any further. It won't work if it's her idea. She's already lost trust. They need to think they came up with this all on their own.

***

Everyone is still talking and laughing in the living room as the day turns into evening. Barbara looks out the kitchen window and sees Hooley on the front steps, looking at his phone. She grabs her coat from a hook. As she opens the door, he looks back at her over his shoulder.

"Mrs. Shaw."

"You okay out here?"

"I'm waiting for Lisa. We're going on a donut run. You want something?"

"Oh, I couldn't eat another thing," she lies as she sits on the step above him.

"My mom always said I was a bottomless pit."

"A pretty good match for a pregnant woman."

He laughs. They sit quietly.

"I thought you might be mad at me," Barbara says.

"Mad at you?"

"I heard my meddling didn't really work out."

"Oh, *that*." His laughter sounds hollow. "Nope. Didn't go over as well as we hoped."

She wants to tell him it's Julie's loss, but it feels disloyal. "I shouldn't have stuck my nose in." It's close to an apology.

"No, you know what? I needed to get it off my chest. Now I'm free to move on."

"Okay, then. I'm glad."

"You were right. It didn't end up the way you planned."

Lisa comes to the door then. He stands and offers his hand to help her on the stairs. Barbara holds the door, then slips back inside. She watches from the kitchen as he opens the passenger door, and Lisa climbs into his truck. He says something and she laughs. Barbara can't hear what he has said.

They drive away, and Barbara heads back toward the living room. Jenna is coming down the hall. "I'm going to need you to watch Will and Ruby tonight," she says.

Barbara tips her head, unused to the spontaneity. Jenna is a planner.

And then, quietly, calmly: "My water broke."

Chapter Twelve

In the morning, Will and Ruby wake early and watch cartoons until Barbara gets up to make them breakfast. She has no text messages from Jenna or Sam and doesn't want to bother them in case they've managed to catch a brief nap within the whirlwind of labor.

"They'll call as soon as there's news," she tells the children, but the moment the words are in the air, she begins to doubt the sentiment. That's how it was with Will and Ruby, but would everything work out the same with this baby? Maybe they'd call Liam and Marco first, then Liam's mother, Nancy. Barbara wonders how far down the phone tree she has fallen.

Will gets permission to take his bowl of cereal back down the hall to eat in front of the television. Ruby climbs into a seat at the kitchen table across from her grandmother.

With Will, the labor started in the middle of the night. Sam had called from Jenna's phone, and Barbara heard the panic in his voice. With Ruby, Jenna went into labor in the middle of a family therapy session in her home office. She finished the session, texted Barbara to pick Will up from school, and waited for Sam on the front stoop with her hospital bag at her feet.

Both had come early, but labor was long. Not this long.

Barbara taps the surface of her cell phone on the table. Ruby endlessly stirs her oatmeal.

"Not hungry?"

"My tummy hurts." Ruby is pouting, staring into her bowl.

"Your tummy hurts?"

She nods without making eye contact.

"Are you worried about your mom?"

She lifts her tiny shoulders, lets them fall.

Barbara reminds herself that, although this is her third time, it's Ruby's first. "You don't have to worry. These things can take a while. Mommies have been doing this since the beginning of time." She leaves out the fact that some—many, have died. But she reminds herself it's rare for that to happen these days. "Do you know how long we waited for *you*?"

Ruby sighs. Barbara can tell she's not interested in this story.

"Honey, what's wrong?"

Ruby chews her bottom lip, thinking. Barbara waits, holding her breath.

"Do you think Uncle Liam will stop liking me now because he has his own baby to take home?"

"Oh, Ruby!" Lisa cries out from the doorway. She's wearing a blue nightgown that falls at her knees, her braids wrapped in a silk scarf of yellow flowers.

"Of course not," Barbara says quickly, though, if she's honest, the thought has occurred to her. This is another reason she's not always honest.

Lisa steps into the kitchen, kneels beside Ruby's chair, and wraps the girl in her arms. Hugging an adult with her big belly might be awkward, but Ruby presses herself into the extra padding.

"I know for a fact that can't happen." Lisa pulls back and looks into Ruby's eyes. "I had a long talk with Liam last night about how much he loves being a part of your family and how crazy he is about you. I'm sure the new baby will win a place in his heart, but you've already got yours."

Ruby's sad face disappears like it had never been there. She grins and turns to Barbara for confirmation.

"Well, there you have it. A fact." She reaches across the table to touch the tip of Ruby's nose. "Okay?"

Ruby nods.

Barbara gets up to help Lisa stand. "Go watch cartoons with your brother. I'll bring you a warm bowl of oatmeal."

Ruby runs down the hall, and Lisa takes her seat at the table. Barbara takes the bowl of cold oatmeal to the trash. Starting over.

"Did Liam convince you an open adoption is the way to go?" Not that it matters now. Barbara's Hail Mary pass has been intercepted by Jenna's broken water. There's no time to make Liam consider Lisa's baby instead. She's glad now she never suggested it out loud. "Actually, no."

"No?"

"Not an open adoption. Not a closed adoption." Barbara puts Ruby's bowl in the microwave, scowling. She sets the time, wondering what new option has been created for unintended pregnancies.

"I'm not giving him up."

Barbara turns. "What?"

"I'm going to be his mom."

Barbara feels the kind of joy she can't remember feeling since Jenna first told her she was pregnant all those months ago. She sits across from Lisa and takes her hands. "You are?"

Lisa nods, looking down.

"Congratulations!"

Lisa looks up, uncertain. "Yeah?"

"Oh, yes!"

"You don't think I'll be a horrible mother?"

"Don't be silly. You're going to be great. Look at what you did for Ruby. I had no idea what I was going to say. But you were perfect."

Lisa melts against the back of her chair, letting out a long exhale. "I told her the truth. Man, oh man, the way Liam's face lights up when he talks about her. If every child had one person in their life who loved them so much, the world would be a better place."

"And your child will have that, too." Barbara feels this authentically, but she can't help feeling something else. This is the wrong baby to be kept. Another thing that didn't end up the way she had planned.

The microwave beeps. She glances at her phone. It's after nine. She brings Ruby her breakfast and sends a quick text to Sam she hopes sounds breezy and not impatient. Nagging. Worried.

***

An hour later, Stewart's car pulls into the drive. Barbara hasn't heard from Jenna or Sam. She's washing the breakfast dishes in the sink, despite having a perfectly good dishwasher. She sets the last spoon in the dish drainer as Stewart walks up the front steps and waves to her in the window.

"Any news?" he asks as he comes inside.

Barbara shakes her head.

"These things take time," Ruby says without looking up from her coloring book.

"Well, aren't you smart?"

"Yeah, I wonder where you heard this," Barbara says, snapping a dishtowel in her direction.

Ruby giggles, looking up. Her eyes settle on Stewart, and her face falls as she remembers. "I'm sorry about Trudy. Are you very sad?"

Stewart sits without taking off his jacket. "Yes, I suppose I am. Trudy was a special girl."

Ruby nods and pats his hand, solemnly.

Barbara gives the moment a beat before announcing Stewart is taking her to get donuts. His eyebrows lift but he gets to his feet. She pretends to take orders and leaves Lisa in charge. After he starts the car, she turns to him. "I need you to drive me to the hospital."

***

Stewart doesn't go inside the hospital with her. Jenna won't want to see him right now; he'll wait until she's home and situated.

Situated. Barbara thinks of what this means. With Will and Ruby, this meant a visit to Jenna's house a few days after she was discharged. The baby would be pink and tiny, swallowed up by one of the brand-new outfits from the baby shower. Jenna would be sleep-deprived, sour smelling, sitting on a pillow the hospital sent home, so *happy*.

Barbara has spent months focused on which house the baby would be brought to, she forgot to consider more basic concerns.

She pauses at the hospital entrance, waiting for the *woosh* of the automatic doors signaling the beginning of the sensory experience; this is the hospital where Bill died. No, he hadn't died here, but this was the last place she'd seen him. In a room with a sheet pulled up to his chin, the gray-green pallor of his face suddenly permanent. She kissed his forehead and left the lipstick print there for him to take to the great beyond.

She wonders if Jenna ever thinks of this when she's here, bringing life into the world. If the disinfectant smell triggers thoughts of death or babies.

The lobby has been renovated several times over the years. The front desk has been moved to the center of the room. A round woman with curly, dark hair is occupied with an elderly couple. Barbara brushes past, making a beeline for the elevators, which are right where they've always been.

She presses the button for the third floor without glancing at the directory. All her children have built their lives around fixing things: bodies, minds, and houses. They are all better than her. Wasn't this the goal? They genuinely want to improve the world. Especially Jenna. As a child, she moved earthworms out of the road after rainstorms. That's how big her heart is.

Barbara could build a case if anyone would listen. She'd offer herself in trade, in a heartbeat. She knows it doesn't work that way.

Barbara steps out of the elevator and takes a right into the outer family waiting room. It's empty except for two people. Lost in her thoughts, she nearly passes them on her way to the check-in window. It's a man, huddled, covering his face, a woman bent over him, touching his shoulder.

In a moment, Barbara recognizes the woman. She hadn't seen her for years, the blond bob fading gray, the white coat with her name embroidered in bright blue thread over her left breast: Dr. Bartlett. Jenna's OBGYN.

The man is easier to identify, even with his face covered. He feels as much her son as Billy.

He looks up as she gasps. She can't find the words to ask; she's sure she doesn't want to know.

Sam stands and grasps her by the shoulders as the room tilts. He helps her to a chair. "Jenna's fine," he says, and she stares at him with her mouth open. "Really."

Sam does polite reintroductions, and the doctor takes her leave. Barbara forces herself to take a breath.

"And the baby?"

"The baby too. Everyone's fine."

"You were crying."

"It's been a long night." He looks out the window. "And morning."

There's more, of course. Everyone's fine *now*. He didn't call earlier because he couldn't say this, wasn't sure it would be true. Labor had been exhausting, hours and hours of pain and pacing with little forward motion. All night, things progressed slowly, and then, suddenly, a rush. There was too much bleeding, an emergency c-section. Things were touch-and-go. The baby wasn't breathing at all at first, then wasn't breathing enough or right. And then, when it seemed everyone had weathered the storm, more bleeding. A hysterectomy.

"She wasn't planning to do this again, but it's still a tough pill to swallow."

Barbara nods. "Is she sleeping?"

"I left her with Julie." He lifts his arms as if to defend against the coming barrage. "I didn't call her either. She said she *knew*."

Barbara's arms are covered in goosebumps. She remembers getting the call at work when Jenna had to go to the ER for gallbladder pain her freshman year of high school. Julie's junior high had called before she'd left the building.

Julie comes through the door then, and Sam heads back.

"You should go home to sleep," Julie says.

"I will." He shrugs. "Just not yet."

Julie sits down, shaking her head as he leaves. "That man sure does love my sister. I nearly maced him the first time we met. Did I ever tell you the story?"

Barbara laughs. Yes, she remembers. Something about mixing up their cars and thinking he was a carjacker "You were there for their meet cute, how many years ago?" She looks to Julie for the answer, but she has dissolved into tears.

"I fucking hate hospitals!" Julie shouts, wiping her face angrily against her shirt sleeve.

"You must be tired."

"I will never understand why women do this to themselves. If anything had happened to her." She shakes her head and is quiet for a long time, and Barbara thinks this is all she'll say. Then she throws her shoulders back, chin out, and says, almost defiantly: "I got pregnant once. I never told anyone. Not Hooley, not Jenna. No one." She hesitates, bites her lip and seems to wish she hadn't said it.

"I can keep a secret," Barbara says.

Julie rolls her eyes, but she smiles. "I suppose that's true."

Barbara doesn't have to ask when this was. She knows. This was the year she moved back home to get away from Maine, away from Hooley. She had barely spoken to Barbara for years, but she was desperate for somewhere to go, and Barbara was desperate for any excuse to be let back in.

"When I terminated the pregnancy, I knew I couldn't be with him. He never would have forgiven me, but it was a moment of clarity for me, too. I could have had the life he wanted. It was right there. But I didn't want that."

"Wow," Barbara says. "You were brave, even then."

"Brave?" Julie sits forward. "This is *not* what I would have expected you to say."

"I might not have at the time," Barbara admits. Jenna and Sam were married by then, but Will hadn't been born. The first grandbaby. She might not have been able to see past it. She might not have seen the beautiful, independent, tough-as-nails woman Julie already knew she would become.

"Why did you never tell Jenna?"

She shrugs.

Barbara sits silently with the knowledge she has a secret no one else has. Her daughter trusted her alone.

Julie stands then, breaking the moment before it becomes too sentimental. "Let's go force Sam to go home."

***

Convincing Sam to go is harder than she imagined. Barbara promises she'll stay as long as Jenna will have her. Jenna assures him she'll be fine and reminds him someone will have to pick up their children. Julie actually has to pull him by the arm after he has kissed his wife on the forehead, the hand, the lips.

"He thought he might lose you," Barbara says, sitting in the chair Sam has pulled close to the bed.

Jenna dismisses this with a quick shake of her head. "He's being dramatic."

Barbara raises a dubious eyebrow but doesn't push it. "How's your pain?"

"It's not bad."

Barbara's face remains dubious.

"Morphine." Jenna lifts the arm attached to the IV.

"Good." Barbara nods. "How's the baby?"

"He's perfect," she says. "He looks exactly like Ruby." Her eyes fill with tears, but through some amazing trick of physics or sheer will, they do not overflow. Her eyes widen as the tears are trapped within, and somehow, it feels rude to acknowledge them. Jenna seems to think if she can keep tears from overflowing, they'll both be able to pretend this isn't happening.

After a long moment of precarious silence, a single tear escapes, sliding slowly down the side of her nose. Barbara stands to retrieve a box of tissues from a table near the window.

"Where is he?"

"I made Liam take him to the nursery. It was killing me to be around him. Don't gloat, please."

"Gloat?" Barbara holds out the tissues, and Jenna takes the entire box.

"You said I wouldn't be able to do this."

"What do I know?" Barbara was always cautioning her. In college, Jenna had spent weeks under mosquito netting in Peru despite Barbara's hysterical protests. When she chose the bright watermelon paint for the bath, Barbara said it would be too much, over the top. Months into her fertility treatment for Ruby, Barbara begged her to stop, but Jenna never listened. Barbara advised, and Jenna ignored.

The bathroom turned out beautiful. The paint picked up the colors of jungle flowers in the series of framed photographs. It could have been in an interior design magazine. And Ruby was one of the best things about being alive.

"You told me you knew this was going to be hard," Barbara says.

Jenna groans, curling into a ball, hugging the box of tissues to her chest. "But it's *so* hard."

"Well, I suppose you don't exactly have a blueprint for this sort of thing, do you? The downside to the *road less traveled* they never tell you about."

"I feel like my heart is being ripped from my body."

"Some of that is hormones." Barbara remembers when Bill came to the hospital after the twins were born. Crazed with hormones, worried about her soul, she'd sent him away like an idiot, sentencing them both to years of unhappiness.

"I thought this is what you wanted." Jenna spits the words out, miserably, and Barbara tries not to let her see how much this stings. To be entirely misunderstood. She doesn't wish this kind of pain on an enemy, never mind a beloved child.

"If you want to take the baby and run, I'll be your getaway driver."

"I would never do that to Liam."

Barbara sighs. "Of course, you wouldn't. We love Liam. He's family."

"I'm afraid I may never feel whole again."

"Oh, you will."

"How do you know?"

"Because I'm your mother, and I know you. You can do anything. This has always been true. I wasn't on board for your vision at the beginning, but I've started to see."

"What do you see?"

"I see you'll go home tomorrow to a man who loves you more than his life and two of the sweetest, happiest children ever made." Barbara sits back down and holds Jenna's wrists, forcing her to stop tearing the tissue to bits. "In a few days, Liam and Marco will bring the baby over. Sometimes it might hurt, but this will be outweighed by love, and we will figure out how to get through as a family."

"Are you sure?" Jenna asks.

"I am," Barbara says, and it's the kindest lie she's ever told.

***

Barbara waits for Jenna to fall asleep before heading to the nursery. On her way, she comes across Liam's mother at a vending machine.

"How's she doing?" Nancy asks, bending to retrieve a Snickers bar.

"Sleeping."

"Oh, good. She earned it."

Barbara doesn't want to talk to this woman about what Jenna has earned. "I wanted to pop my head into the nursery. I won't stay long."

"They're not in the nursery. They put us in a little family room. Come with me and I'll show you."

She follows Nancy down the hall and around the corner. Outside the door, Nancy pauses. "I'm not going in 'cause I'm trying to give them a break." Her voice shifts to a stage whisper: "*From me!*" She laughs at her own joke. "But seriously, I was hoping I'd get to see you today because I wanted to tell you," she reaches out and takes both of Barbara's hands, "I've been where you are."

Barbara smiles and pulls her hands free, slowly. The word that comes to mind: *presumptuous.*

"I hope we can do this together better than we did last time. You're already handling this better than I did. You're here."

It's a generous thing to say, and Barbara feels herself softening, involuntarily. They exchange cell phone numbers for grandmother emergencies—Barbara is the one who suggests this, but she'll never admit it.

Inside, Marco is stretched out on a couch with the baby asleep on his chest. Liam is sitting in an overstuffed turquoise chair, filming with his cell phone. When Barbara pushes slowly through the door, he jumps to his feet, and

Marco starts to sit up, shifting the baby cautiously, holding him up by the armpits as he yawns and squawks, then tucking him into the crook of his arm and watching him settle.

"Already a natural," Barbara says, dodging an incoming hug from Liam and sliding into the newly open seat on the couch next to Marco.

Liam sits in the chair closest to her and asks after Jenna. She pats his hand. "She's going to be fine." She says this looking into his eyes. Then she looks past Marco at the baby, and she is unable to see anything else for many moments. He does look like Ruby, the full lips, long lashes, mass of dark hair. "Does he have a name yet?

"Actually, we wanted to talk to you about that," Marco says.

Barbara reaches out to brush the wisps of dark hair across the baby's forehead. "Me?"

"Ruby was named for my grandmother," Liam says. "My mother's mother."

Barbara hadn't known that. Nancy never said. She leans in closer to take in the new baby smell, captivated by his tiny perfect fingers curled into tiny fists, the tinier fingernails. She's amazed all over again at what the human body is capable of, that her daughter has created this entire little person, all on her own.

"We want to do something similar here, but wanted to be sure you'd approve.," Marco says.

"Oh, dear. My father's name was Frank. He always hated it, though. I don't think he'd wish that on a child of today."

Liam laughs. "No, we were thinking James. Or Jamie."

Barbara's head snaps up then, looking at Liam as if for the first time.

He smiles. "A family name."

***

On her way out of the hospital, Barbara texts Stewart to pick her up, but she sees his car parked in the same spot where he'd dropped her off. He has rolled down his windows.

"Have you been here all along?"

He looks up from his book. *The Condition*. By the placement of his bookmark, he seems to be a few chapters ahead of her. "Such a nice day, and you seemed more worried than you were letting on."

She gets into the front seat and tells him everyone's okay. On the drive home, she tells him the rest. It's a long story, and she leaves some parts out: the secrets she's promised to keep, the complicated feelings that are hers alone. She tells him Julie was there, and she'd taken Sam home. Jenna would stay another night. The baby is healthy, a boy named James. When Stewart eases his car into her driveway and moves to pull out the key, she reaches to still his hand, not sure if he will be staying, if he'll want to come inside. "I need to talk to you."

He turns to her, his eyebrows knit.

"I was not an only child."

"Okay." Stewart is quiet for a long time. "Why did you tell me you were?"

"It's what I was taught to say. It's the story I've been telling for nearly sixty years."

"And what's the true story?"

"I had a little brother." She smiles through her tears, picturing his grin, his chubby cheeks.

"What was he like?"

She considers this; she hasn't tried to put it into words for so long. "He was very clever," she says. "And he was always trying to get people to laugh. He was good at it."

Stewart nods and waits for more.

"And curious. He liked snails and hermit crabs and star fish. We used to play in the tidepools."

"How old were you?"

"I was eight. He was three."

She's quiet, and he reaches for her, pulling her against his chest. She sobs in his arms as if the wound is fresh, unable to remember the last time she let herself cry for James like this or if she ever had. "I always thought it was my fault, Thought my mother agreed. We were never close afterwards. She was never the same. His death broke my family forever."

"I'm sorry." He holds her until the tears stop. She pulls away, wipes her face.

"My children only learned about James recently. After my mother died. Jenna must have told Liam. And now—" She falters, lifts her arms with uncertainty.

"And now, life goes on." Stewart squeezes her hand.

In a few moments, they will go inside. Will and Ruby will never ask for the donuts, and Barbara will never know if it's forgetfulness, or if they're being polite. Sam will come over for dinner, and then he will bring the children back to sleep in their own beds. Stewart will sleep over.

Tomorrow, Barbara will begin moving in with Stewart. He'll give her half the drawers in his bureau, an empty nightstand, most of the closet. She will bring all her business suits to Goodwill. By the time Lisa's baby is born, the move will be complete. Oliver will seem miserable at first, but by the third day, he will claim the sunny windowsill of the living room bay as his favorite spot, as if it has always been so.

But tonight, Barbara will bring Stewart into the room she shared with Bill. She will not think of Bill, but she won't *not* think of Bill. She will let herself think of him or not think of him without feeling like either is a betrayal. Her love for Stewart is not a threat to that love. Bill's love is what makes all other love possible.

Chapter Thirteen

As it turns out, getting permission to bury cremains is not a problem after all. Barbara remembers the hot day in August, has pictures on her phone of everyone at the beach in Maine: Jenna, Sam, Julie, Billy, Liam, Marco, Jamie, Ruby, Will, Toby, Lisa, Monique, Stewart. The family she has because of other people's bravery—maybe some of hers, too.

Billy handled all the arrangements with Father Gregory. There might have been a donation, but he never said so. The little boy priest managed a touching eulogy about the sweet, funny boy James had been, and the man he might have become if he'd been able to grow up. Not a dry eye in the Catholic cemetery.

Barbara will never know exactly how James died. Since her talk with Lisa, she has remembered several different versions. She grew up feeling like her mother blamed her, but maybe her mother's guilt caused her to lash out. Stewart pointed out Barbara would never hold any other eight-year-old child responsible for what she has spent a lifetime blaming her eight-year-old self for. She's trying to let it go. Having people who will remind her helps.

Lisa and Toby had ridden up from Manchester with Barbara and Stewart. In the rear-view mirror, Barbara watched Lisa fuss over a squirming three-month-old. She was much calmer than Barbara had been as a new mother.

She didn't always know right away why he was crying, but she didn't get frantic about it, didn't seem to have those unreachable expectations for herself. She couldn't find his pacifier in the diaper bag and gave him her knuckle. That did the trick.

When Lisa confessed her mother was never really in jail, Barbara pretended not to already know. She encouraged her to get back in touch before the baby was born. Sue was able to be there for the birth, and though she was a reluctant grandmother, she seemed to know it beat the alternative. Barbara knows how long this journey can take, and it's worth every difficult moment.

She sits in the bed next to Stewart now, scrolling through the photos. She's looking for one in particular.

"Julie's coming up on Friday," she reminds him.

He sets the book in his lap. "Down." "Oh." She shakes her head, smiling. "Right."

On Friday night, they're going to the Back Room to celebrate Julie's engagement.

They'd gone back to the house after the cemetery and exchanged their funeral attire for bathing suits. Will and Billy raced into the frigid water as Jenna and Lisa spread blankets, Liam and Ruby shared a bottle of sunscreen, Marco and Julie carried a cooler down from the house, Stewart and Monique held the babies, Sam brought a picnic basket from the car, and Barbara took photos.

The picnic basket was full of store-bought sandwiches Barbara didn't pretend she'd made by hand. She's stopped lying about things that don't matter to people who do. It's easier not doing things she has to lie about.

Now, she finds the photo she's looking for. Henri. He's an architect. He and Julie met at a seminar on universal design in Quebec. They'd done the long-distance thing for an undisclosed amount of time, and now he was moving to Boothbay so they could be together *for real.*

Those were the words Julie had used to describe it, breathless and googly eyed as she is in this photo. Her blond hair is loose, blowing in a breeze as she gazes at him. Barbara had taken the photo covertly.

"Doesn't she look happy?" she asks Stewart.

"She does." He puts his hand on her thigh. It's warm through the covers.

Barbara is getting used to the right side of the bed.

She isn't sure there will be a wedding, per say, and she doesn't care. This might be one of those permanent engagements meant to signify a forever commitment, government paperwork be damned. She finds it hard to picture Julie as a bride. Even when she'd been one, the wedding was accomplished without pageantry, in the courthouse in Portland.

But maybe this time is different. Those googly eyes sure are new.

"Who else is coming?" Stewart asks.

"Jenna and Sam. Liam and Marco. Hooley and Lisa."

"How modern."

Barbara scrolls backward on her phone. Hooley had met them at the beach after the memorial for James. He sat beside Lisa and reached for the baby, lifting him with the comfort of a man who'd done it a hundred times, and Barbara realized they were a couple.

When Barbara moved out of the house, Lisa moved downstairs and turned the den into a nursery, swapping the couch for a crib. She kept Bill's blue recliner in the corner for midnight feedings. She still pays rent, and Barbara puts the money away in a secret account. She thinks of it as Toby's college fund so Lisa will be less likely to refuse it.

She has several images of the babies sitting together in the damp sand, propped up by towels and blankets and each other. The water was too cold for them, and they watched Ruby build sandcastles as the adults tried to keep them from eating the building material. The baby boys are close in age, Barbara likes to imagine them growing up together, like cousins. She had never had cousins; neither had her children. The closest Will and Ruby will get to having a cousin is Jamie. While they are pushing the boundaries of what family can be, why not include Toby?

Stewart sets his book on the nightstand and snaps off his light. "Excited for tomorrow?"

Her stomach somersaults. "Mostly."

In the morning, they're going to see a litter of Labrador puppies. It's a compromise between his suggestion of a Saint Bernard and hers of a cocker spaniel. He doesn't want to walk a prissy ball of fluff wearing a sweater; she doesn't want to walk an excitable puppy that can pull her over.

"Don't tell Oliver."

She groans at the thought. Stewart snickers.

For the first time in her life, she considers getting a pet that could possibly outlive her, and this had forced her to consider mortality in a new way. Her mother lived into her eighties, and Stewart's dad is still going. She decides she can't plan for the worst. She must enjoy the moments she has left.

Sometimes, life seems short, but the truth is, life is long. Barbara is grateful for the time she's had to make things up for her children. She often thinks she might never do enough, but she has come quite far. There were years when her daughters were lost to her, when she didn't have a current address for Julie, and Jenna had to force herself to sit across the table from her. Now, she is invited to celebrate their great joys, trusted to keep their secrets, and counted on to listen to their heartaches.

The best photo is at the end. Jenna laughing with her head tipped back, eyes closed, mouth open. Barbara doesn't remember what was said or who said it, but she can still hear it, the music.

Stewart's breathing steadies, and Barbara is jealous of how fast he falls asleep. She fixes her pillows and lays back.

Men often die before women, and although she knows this will hurt her more than she can bear to think about, the possibility doesn't make her afraid to stay. It only makes staying matter more. Someday, there will be pain. Until then, there will be time.

Acknowledgements

This book took a while to finish. I was writing it during the pandemic when it seemed like everyone else was being so productive and I was endlessly stuck. So the people I'd like to thank are my friends who asked, "How is the book coming?' for all those years when it just wasn't: Kim, Debbie, Rob, Reed, Karen, Pablo, Mary, and more. It really did help to be reminded that I am a writer, and you expected me to finish. Thanks for believing in me.

About The Author

Katie grew up in New Hampshire, went to college in Massachusetts, and settled down in Arizona. These are the environments you'll find in her stories because she thinks having an authentic sense of place is so important when you're reading.

She's been calling herself a writer since the second grade when her teacher had the class bind their stories with patterned paper and put them on display in the library. She writes the kind of fiction she likes to read: character-driven, relationship-focused, and emotionally complex. She has published several novels and a collection of short stories.

She's spent the last twenty years in Tucson where she lives with her sweet yellow lab and even sweeter boyfriend.

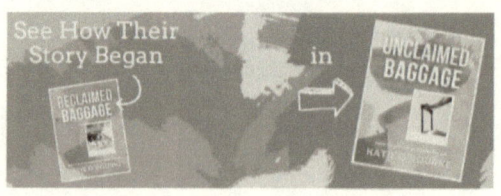

www.ingramcontent.com/pod-product-compliance
Lightning Source LLC
Chambersburg PA
CBHW020149120726
47903CB00007B/2479